William Lane

The correspondents

an original novel, in a series of letters

William Lane

The correspondents
an original novel, in a series of letters

ISBN/EAN: 9783742834294

Manufactured in Europe, USA, Canada, Australia, Japa

Cover: Foto ©Andreas Hilbeck / pixelio.de

Manufactured and distributed by brebook publishing software
(www.brebook.com)

William Lane

The correspondents

THE
CORRESPONDENTS,

AN
ORIGINAL NOVEL,

IN
A SERIES OF LETTERS.

A NEW EDITION.

LONDON:

PRINTED FOR T. BECKET, PALL-MALL,
AND
WILLIAM LANE, LEADENHALL-STREET.
MDCCLXXXIV.

CORRESPONDENTS.

To *.

I KNOW too well the melancholy reafon of your prefent filence, and do not prefume to interrupt it, or defire you to write till perfectly convenient; but the confideration of this day's beginning a *New Year*, induces me to fend you my beft wifhes (not my compliments) on that occafion.

I am juft returning from church, and there, with the moft ardent fincerity,

B   I peti-

I petitioned that your valuable life might be prolonged beyond the common date of humanity; that your fenfibility might never more be wounded by the lofs of a friend; that you might enjoy uninterrupted health and every fpecies of happinefs.

To * *.

I HAVE no fuitable return for your moft kind wifh. The fecond article includes every thing; and is the beft condolence I have received; for on thefe occafions little to the purpofe can be faid.

As

As to the reſt, when I enjoy health I
am thankful; but there are not many
ſpecies of happineſs that I *can* enjoy.
People in advanced life, as their con-
nexions diſſolve, grow indifferent, and
find their attachment to the world de-
creaſe daily: the few pleaſures they can
reliſh, may generally be ſafely afforded
them.   Your correſpondence is numbered among the few that *I* regard:
you will continue it to me, and accept
my ſincere acknowledgments.

To *.

IT is not probable that I ſhall ever
decline a correſpondence that does
me ſo much honour; eſpecially whilſt

I con-

I continue to obferve your indulgent command, of writing " the very firft thoughts that occur when I take up a pen."

I have been amufing myfelf thefe two hours with a piece of embroidery. This eafy occupation engages the fingers without confining the thoughts; fo, after a variety of ideas had ran through my mind, I began on a fudden to review my paft life.

I contempted the chequered fcene with ftrict attention; and concluded at length, that the white hours were infinitely more than the dark in number; and that, far from repining, I had abundant caufe of thankfulnefs to that good Providence whofe bounty had exceeded

my

my defert. Cafting my eyes round, finding myfelf in a very comfortable re-treat—independent of the world—en-joying *tolerable* health—a few friends ftill fpared to me—O *Memory*, thought I, what but *thy* annihilation is wanting to my happinefs! then I could enjoy thefe various bleffings without the re-flection of their uncertainty, without the dread of their fudden lofs.—Here I broke off my meditation, and endea-voured to confirm my tranquillity, by communicating this account of it, which I know will afford a generous fatisfac-tion to your benign heart; a fatisfaction that may increafe, by your recollecting to *whofe* advice and affiftance I am principally indebted for that indepen-dence which is my chief boaft.

You

You have forbidden achnowledg-
ments; yet allow me this once to fpeak
my grateful remembrance of the obligation, and fubfcribe myfelf, with the.
utmoft refpeɛt,

Your moft devoted, &c.

To * *.

THE fubftance of your letter is a
very agreeable leffon in moral philofophy; but I wifh you had omitted the
conclufion. How often muft I repeat
that you owe me no obligation? The
aɛt of rendering you a fmall fervice was
its own reward; and the endeavouring
to improve our acquaintance into friendfhip

fhip was to pleafe myfelf. Why then
do we not converfe upon equal terms?
Why any *refpeƐ? the utmoſt refpeƐ*, my
moſt devoted? How am I to account for
the ufe of thefe terms? Can the trifling
and accidental difference of our *rank*
make any impreffion on your mind?—
Impoffible!—Your foul is undoubtedly
fuperior to that weaknefs.

T *.

I SHOULD be very forry if you
afcribed the marks of my *refpeƐful*
efteem to a wrong motive; and think
my foul *is* fuperior to the weaknefs you
mention.

I *may*

I *may* seem occasionally humble; a profound veneration *does* sometimes make an impreſſion on my mind; but it is *character*, not *rank*, which excites that humility and veneration.—You may remember conducting me much nearer the meridian ſplendor of *title*; but you do not remember that I was dazzled by its rays.—The *higheſt* rank, if unaccompanied by that extenſive genius, thoſe exalted talents, that long and improved acquaintance with the world, that perfect and univerſal knowledge of men and things, which unite to form the character of a certain perſon, could never exact from me that reſpect which I cheriſh for *him*; and which is not leſſened by his acquittal of my numerous obligations.

To

To * *.

IF you have not justified yourself at the expence of your sincerity, it is all very well: but

> " O beware, beware of *Flattery* !
> " It is a monster, that like Jealousy,
> " Doth make the meat it feeds on."—

Long life, as the gift of providence, is valuable, if employed to advantage; but an acquaintance with the world, a knowledge of mankind, can very seldom procure either respect or happiness. " He that increaseth knowledge, in-" creaseth sorrow." Again, says *the Preacher*, " I considered all travel and " every right work, that for this a man " is envied of his neighbour. Of " making many books there is no end;

" and

" and much ftudy is wearinefs." I cannot think of thefe things, nor of the
various experiments which I, like *him*,
have unfuccefsfully made to obtain happinefs, without drawing the fame penfive conclufion, that *all is vanity*.

You fuppofe me well acquainted with
the world. I *have* feen fomething of
it ; enough to be almoft tired, fince novelty has loft its charms. New fa-
fhions, new cuftoms, new opinions, are
daily ftarting up. I cannot adopt them
with the facility of youth. I weigh,
ponder, examine, perhaps rejeft, them.
The world, that world I am fo perfeftly
acquainted with—derides me as an ob-
ftinate old fellow, for declining its prefent mode ; but pays no kind of regard
to my ufelefs experience. Every age
thinks

thinks itfelf wifer than the former; the improvements of every age confirm this idea. Take care you become not fo unfafhionable, as to regard any thing but the accomplifhments, the wit, the elegance, the genius, of the prefent hour!

To *.

YOUR laft letter had very nearly put a period to our correfpon-dence. " *All is vanity !" You are almoft tired of the world!* I neither doubt it, nor wonder, becaufe there are fo few things, and fo few people in it, that can poffibly amufe or engage a mind like your's. What prefumption in *me* to at-

tempt either!—It is with reluctance I
fend this.   Could I but know the time,
the place, the circumstances, the difpofition, in which you received my notes
—but to intrude and break in upon
your more important thoughts with fuch
frivolous infignificance! — Perhaps the
very inftant of reading this was devoted
to a better employment.   Why do I fay
perhaps? there is no doubt of it.   Pardon therefore the interruption; and refume (before it is wholly broken) the
thread of your contemplation.

To

To * *.

I WAS in a very ill humour, had company with me, and had juſt done dinner, when your letter was brought. Ten times more frivolous than that was the converſation it interrupted; ſo I read it over again and again, till at length it produced a change in my temper. Your amiable and generous ſolicitude to pleaſe *me*, inſpired *me* with an inclination to pleaſe *my gueſts*. In proportion as my endeavours ſucceeded, my cheerfulneſs increaſed; every body ſeemed to improve; and the evening went off with tolerable ſatisfaction.

So, for this time, becauſe of the good effect they had on me, I pardon your diffidence, your doubts, ſcruples, and

apo-

apologies; but repeat them not, I conjure you. Believe, that all times, in all places and circumſtances, your letters will be acceptable. Herewith I return you a pacquet, (October and December incluſive) and, to ſatisfy you ſtill farther, will in future delay open-ing them till the proper moment of leiſure.

Adieu! if you now perſiſt in apolo-gies, you are not the perſon I take you for.

To *.

YOU are not difpleafed with me?
I am and will be the perfon you
take me for: but indeed you could not
have chofen a worfe time for the refto-
ration of my letters. I have been reading them over as I burnt them, and am
put entirely out of conceit with myfelf.
Such low, trifling, ridiculous ftuff; and
above all, fuch a feeming imitation of
your ftyle and manner—Yet I proteft it
is not an imitation.—Don't laugh at my
vanity.—I mean only *that* ftyle (very
different from other writing) in which
you honour me with a familiar correfpondence.

I remember you were angry at fuch
an obfervation once before; but I cannot

not help being ftill of opinion, that
this mode of expreffion, particularly the
fhort and interrogatory fentences, however fuitable to you, do very ill become
your correfpondent.

To * *.

WHEN I firft propofed this friendly correfpondence, you pleaded
inability to maintain it ; upon which, I
promifed never to write or require long
or correct letters. A few artlefs lines,
expreffive of health, of friendfhip, of
any thing but ftudy and affectation, was
all that I requefted from you, or gave
you to expect from me.

I eftablifhed

I eftablifhed at the fame time a very unexceptionable *conveyance*; and promifed to return your letters: in fhort, according to my notion of things, I removed every objeftion that diffidence, difcretion, or delicacy could fuggeft.

Your letter intimates the contrary. You are now diffatisfied becaufe there appears a fimilarity in our ftyle.—Have I not already told you, that when two perfons of fimilar—but I hate repetitions—your next letter will decide the point. If you chufe to difcontinue the correfpondence, I fhall readily acquiefce: but pray do not give yourfelf the trouble of writing any more excufes.

To

To *.

MAY I venture to write at all? for now you are indeed ferioufly angry, and with reafon. Forgive me this once, and I will endeavour to merit your forgivenefs.

We have had feveral new plays this winter;—but I fuppofe you have read them all.—*Two* I know are publifhed, *Zingis* and *Cyrus*, which laft I faw a few nights ago, and was extremely well entertained.

You muft allow me to confine my criticifm entirely to the *performance*, which I thought remarkably happy.— Mrs. *Yates* was amazingly great; the part is quite in her caft; fhe was charm-
ingly

ingly dreffed, preferved the idea of
royalty through every fcene, and in
every different attitude *looked* a *Mandane.* Mr. *Powell* too pleafed me exceedingly; his perfon was greatly favoured in a fingular and very becoming
drefs; and I thought I difcovered feveral new beauties in his action. He
drew tears from me without fpeaking a
word, in that fcene where his mother
urges him to acknowledge himfelf her
fon; and he with infinite emotion de-
clines the explanation. Thefe tears
were all I fhed. I am feldom much
affected by pompous declamation, or
high-wrought paffion; and the poet
had well nigh forfeited my pity for
Mandane, by painting her fo favage in
her revenge.

I was

I was pleafed with two circumftances in the exhibition of this piece, which I never remember to have feen before; one was, the ftage being wholly covered with green cloth, which appeared quite proper, as the fcene lies without doors; and prevented the abfurdity of bringing carpets to fall upon: — the other was, feeing Mrs. *Yates*, in a fuppofed agony of terror, fall motionlefs to the ground without affiftance.—The audience in general applauded this manœuvre; and feemed fenfible how much better an effect it had, than her being caught by attendants, whofe unmeaning faces would probably have fpoiled the fcene.

Enough at this time for the patience of my noble reader, who will now, I hope,

hope, fign a free pardon for his reform-
ed and penitent correfpondent.

—————————————————————————

To * *.

YOUR pardon is undoubtedly fign-
ed, fealed, and delivered;—but I
cannot greatly admire the epithet you
beftow on me, and muft beg leave to
difclaim it. It is not your noble reader,
but your friend, your good friend, who
returns thanks for your letter; and was
very well pleafed with your criticifm—
Come then, let us hear a little more of
the matter. Let us know what you *are*
affeéted by in dramatic reprefentation,
if not by declamation or paffion: alfo
what fpecies of theatrical entertainment
you

you prefer to the reſt. Here is a large
field, from which I expeçt a copious
harveſt. Adieu!

Your's very ſincerely.

_____

To *.

THE field may be large, and the
harveſt great; yet the labourer
may not have ſtrength to reap it. But
this is not an apology; for I enter very
cheerfully upon my taſk.

My theatrical taſte, then, (without
farther preface) has undergone ſeveral
revolutions. When I was about half
my preſent age, I admired nothing but
pantomime,

pantomime, and the agile tricks of Harlequin, though, at the same time, prompted by childish vanity, I affected to despise them. Soon after that period, my taste really altered. *Romeo* and *Alexander* became my heroes. I was pleased with alternate sighing and storming; and the most extravagant scenes of the most extravagant tragedies appeared to me the noblest and most delightful. Weaned from this folly, I took a strong fancy to *musical* pieces, on account of performing them on my own instruments; then ascending, as I thought, a full scale in the climax of refinement, nothing would please me but the *Italian* opera: this, however, was a short-liv'd passion; and was succeeded by a fondness of the historical drama, and those plays that are usually

classed

claffed under the title of *genteel comedy*;
and thefe, with a few exceptions, continue my favourite entertainments. Re-
garding the theatres as the mirror of human life, I prefer fuch pieces as reflect
in my notions the moft agreeable reprefentations of it: from hence arifes my
admiration of Shakfpeare. I have no
time to confider how he ftrains probability in his *events*, my attention is
wholly engaged by the innumerable
ftrokes of truth and nature in his *characters*. How amiable, how interefting
are fome of thefe! I am not going to
write a panegyric on this immortal bard,
but I fhall for ever love and honour his
memory, becaufe he is the only poet
(that I know of) who has delineated to
perfection the character of a *female
friend*. Now, if to this fome *manly* critic

tic fhould *wittily* objeſt, that Shakefpeare created many *imaginary beings,* I will readily allow *that,* becaufe it does not affeſt this charaſter. We *wonder* at the fairies, at the witches, at Ariel, at Caliban, but do we wonder at *Celia?* No, fhe is generally paffed over with inattention, which alone is fufficient to prove that the charaſter is not uncommon, at leaft not *unnatural;* but it often proves more, it proves a flownefs in difcovering the beauties of this matchlefs writer.

Pray, pray, now good lords of the creation, let us do juftice to my favourite heroine: while David and Jonathan, Pylades and Oreftes, Damon and Pythias, are fo triumphantly held up on your fide, let us at leaft ereſt one ftandard of friendfhip on our own, and in-

C fcribe

scribe it with the names of Celia and Rosalind.

Consider then, in the first place, the *situation* of these two friends.

" Rosalind, the old Duke's daughter, is not banished with her father ... for ... the new Duke's daughter, her cousin, so loves her, (being from their cradles bred together) that she would have followed her exile, or have died to stay behind her."

Observe too, that *Rosalind* carried the palm of beauty; she was " tall and fair," her cousin, " low and browner." " Thou art a fool;" says the Duke to Celia, " she robs thee of thy name; and thou wilt shew more bright, and seem more virtuous when she is gone."

And

And now let us recollect the conduct and fentiments of this magnanimous girl.

Cel. I pray thee, Rofalind, fweet my coz, be merry.

Rof. Dear Celia, I fhew more mirth than I am miftrefs of; and would you I were yet merrier? Unlefs you can teach me how to forget a banifhed father, you muft not expect me to remember any extraordinary pleafure.

Cel. Herein I fee thou lov'ft me not with the full weight that I love thee. If my uncle, thy banifhed father, had banifhed *my* father, fo *thou* hadft been ftill with me, I could have taught my love to take thy father for mine.

Rof. Well, I will forget the condition of my own eftate to rejoice in your's.

Cel. You know my father hath no child but I, nor none is like to have: and truly, when he dies, thou fhalt be his heir; for what he hath taken away from thy father *per* force, I will ren-

der

der thee again in affection ; by mine honour, I will ;—and when I break that oath let me turn monster : therefore, my sweet Rose, my dear Rose, be merry.

I pass over her generous intercession with the Duke, when his anger breaks out against Rosalind, and shall trouble you only with what immediately follows the sentence of her banishment.

Cel. O, my poor Rosalind ? where wilt thou go ?
I charge thee, be not thou more griev'd than I am.
Ros. I have more cause.
Cel. Thou hast not, Cousin ;
Pr'ythee be cheerful ; know'st thou not the Duke
Hath banish'd *me*, his daughter ?
Ros. That he hath not.
Cel. No ! hath not ? Rosalind lacks then the love
Which teacheth *me* that thou and I are one.
Shall we be sunder'd ? shall we part, sweet girl ?
No ;—let my father seek another heir.

Therefore,

Therefore, devife with me how we may fly,
Whither to go, and what to bear with us;
And do not feek to take your change upon you,
To bear your griefs yourfelf and leave me out:
For *by this heaven,* now at our forrows paie,
Say what thou canft, I'll go along with thee.

The heroic generofity of this refolution, and the fortitude, conftancy, and
cheerfulnefs that attended the execution
of it, made a very early impreffion on
my mind; and from the time I remember any thing, I remember a particular
efteem for the character of Celia. You
will pardon, therefore, my prolixity in
fpeaking of it, and will allow too, I
fancy, that the play in general abounds
with moral, poetical, dramatic, and fen-
timental beauties.

I have

I have now had the honour to acquaint you at large with my theatrical
opinions; for you gather from what I
have faid concerning this comedy, that
I prefer the flow of converfation to the
pomp of declamation; and am more interefted, more affeɛted, and confequent-
ly better pleafed by one Shakefperian
touch of nature and fentiment, than by
all the moft florid and impaffioned
fpeeches of other tragedians.

I have *laughed* at the forrows of *Theo-*
dofius and the ravings of *Roxana*:—I
have *wept* at the generofity of old *Adam,*
and the tendernefs of *Miranda.*

How beautiful her addrefs to Ferdi-
nand!

— Alas

————Alas now, pray you
Work not fo hard ;—Sit down and reft yourfelf.

————If you'll fit down,
I'll bear your logs the while.—Pray give me that,
I'll carry it to the pile.

I fhall not apologife for the length of this fcribble, neither am I fearful of your *thinking* it too long. Your *corrective* letter opened my eyes and my heart. I fee that I have nothing to apprehend. I fee plainly that the happinefs of your friendfhip awaits me; and I accept it with the utmoft gratitude. My *friend,* my *good friend,* I bid you moft refpectfully adieu.

C   To

To * *.

I CANNOT exprefs the fatisfaction your letter gave me. I have been reading it ever fince; and rejoice to difcover in you that elegant *fimplicity* of tafte which is my chief admiration. Your heart was rather tedious in expanding; but you fay it *is* open, and you *accept* my friendfhip. Cherifh, cultivate that friendfhip, and give me your's in return. Be affured that I fhall prize it highly.—I will compare it to a benignant ftar. My fun of happinefs is fet; and the fhades of night cannot be very far diftant; but your friendfhip, like a ftar glimmering in the twilight, fhall illumine and chear my penfive walk through the evening of life.

Adieu.

Adieu. I am coming to town. Do not write till you hear from me: I hope we fhall meet oftener than we did laft year. You do not live wholly at * * * ? I want to fee your place there. Perhaps I may not wait for an invitation. Adieu.

P. S. Is your *ftandard* firm ? or have you recollected you were oppofing fiction to truth ? A word to the wife.—I fhall not prefs the argument. Adieu.

C 5 To

To the fame.

I OWE you a thoufand apologies for yefterday's intrufion. Your *furprife* difconcerted me fo much, that I do not remember what excufes I made. It was certainly very ridiculous ... but finding you were at home and alone, hearing too (as I went up ftairs) the found of a harpfichord, and your voice accompanying, I knew you muft be at leifure, and entered in that abrupt manner, for which I immediately blamed myfelf, and again afk your pardon.

Aceept my thanks too for a more obliging reception than was due to fo rude a gueft. I am charmed with your little villa, its decorations, its furniture, and its miftrefs. The thoughts of them

3   all

all together fpoiled my dinner, and made me repent having declined your *half-invitation*. My curiofity is not fatisfied; I don't know what garden you have: did I fee the extent of it from the dref-fing-room window? Interrupted. Adieu. Pray give me a line *per return*.

To *.

IT was quite unneceffary to take the trouble of *apologifing* for your fudden vifit. I don't know but in fome refpects it was better than otherwife, becaufe I fhall not in future expect—You under-ftand and pardon this freedom, afcrib-ing all to the right motive. Pardon too my not enlarging on the fubject, for

C 6   the

the polite Mrs. ***** (who gives me the honour of taking the air with her this morning) is waiting whilſt I write this. Adieu.

To * *.

WHERE are you, my good friend, and what are you about? I have been theſe three days in hourly expectation of a letter. Your laſt was only an apology for one: ſo cool, ſo conciſe; but I " aſcribed it to the right motive," and thought you would write again. Let me beg that you *will* do ſo immediately. I hope my *viſit* was not *any way* diſagreeable or unſerviceable to the cauſe I wiſhed to promote.

To

To *.

I DELAY not one moment to aſſure you, with the utmoſt ſincerity, that the honour of your viſit was in the high-eſt degree welcome and agreeable; nor was it at all unſerviceable to the cauſe which, I *flatter* myſelf, you deſigned it to promote. I only delayed writing till I ſhould hear again from you, hoping you would give me a new ſubjeƈt, and ſpare me the neceſſity of re-entreating your pardon for declining .... I know not how to expreſs myſelf..... for declining the favour of your par-ticular notice.—You acknowledged on Monday, that my objeƈtions to a per-ſonal intercourſe were not ill-founded; but I need not embarraſs myſelf with arguments.

arguments. I know you will have the goodnefs to acquiefce, and *in filence* too. We *fhall* fometimes fee each other *by accident.* " C'eft affez." Adieu. I fubfcribe myfelf, with pride and pleafure,

Your FRIEND.

To * *.

" I THANK you, I am not of many words, but I thank you †," and hope you will approve my laconic acknowledgment. I am happy that you have at length *fubfcribed* yourfelf my Friend, becaufe I believe your veracity

† Shakefpeare.

unqueftion-

unqueftionable, and have long been co-
veting your friendfhip. Nor will you
be a lofer by the bargain: for this *bribe*
will induce me to *acquiefce* with your
prefent determination, " and in *filence*
too." Ah, my dear Mrs. * *, you
know very well who has the worft end
of the argument.

I am juft at this inftant in tolerable
good humour with all the world; and
having excluded the cares of it for one
half hour, may poffibly contradict the
affertion I began with, and prove myfelf
" of many words:" but thefe little con-
tradictions are always forgiven in a letter. They abound particularly in love-
letters, where an enamoured fwain frequently laughs and cries, burns and
freezes, lives and dies, in the fame
breath,

breath, while the tender nymph, in *her* epiftles, hopes and fears, doubts and believes, rejects and accepts, with equal facility and confiftence.

Let me tell you juft now, before it escapes my memory, that I was mightily pleafed this morning by a very trivial circumftance. It was in turning over a volume of Sterne's Sentimental Journey, (you have read it no doubt) where I was ftruck by the following paffage :

———" I was certain fhe was of a better order of beings—a guarded franknefs with which fhe gave me her hand, fhewed, I thought, her good education and her good fenfe; and as I led her on, I felt a pleafurable ductility about her,

her, which fpread a calmnefs over all my fpirits.——

" I had not yet feen her face—'twas not material—but when we got to the door fhe withdrew her hand from acrofs her forehead——It was a face of about fix-and-twenty (*not quite fo much*) of a clear tranfparent brown, fimply fet off without rouge or powder—it was not *critically* handfome, but there was that in it which attached me much more to it—it was interefting; I fancied it wore the charaĉters of a widowed look, &c. &c. &c.——but you did not know *Sterne*, you did not therefore fit to him for this piĉture.

" Alas, poor Yorick! *I* knew him, Horatia." He was indeed " a fellow of
infinite

infinite jeſt, of moſt excellent fancy."
Pity that his genius was ſo tainted, ſo
impure, the more pity, becauſe his works
will be read.   He ſtrews pearls in a
ditch, and *obliges* his readers to dive for
them.   The ſingle ſtory of *Le Fevre,* if
ſkilfully detached from the life of *Shandy,*
would do immortal honour to his memory ; but it is too firmly incorporated;
and, like the embroidery on *Martin's*
coat, muſt adhere to the main ſtuff, or
be torn to rags †.

Adieu.   I have other letters to write.
Let me hear from you to-morrow ; and
pray give me *your* opinion of this writer,
with a liſt of thoſe chapters which you
prefer to the reſt in his Journey.

† Tale of a Tub.

To

To *.

I WRITE this afternoon becaufe you defired me, though I am in a very unfuitable difpofition, being extremely peevifh, tired, and fatigued, by the per-fecution of a vifit four hours long from Mr. ———. I believe you have heard of him. I had received your letter, and was fitting down to anfwer it the very moment that he came in. I was under the neceffity of afking him to dine—but fuch a dinner! " O gentle Jupiter, with what tedious homilies did he weary my fpirits."—For you muft know this cox-comb is not one of that brifk lively fpe-cies, who engrofs *all* the converfation, (I can bear them well enough) but a grave, folemn one. who paufes—and takes fnuff—and afks impertinent quef-

tions

tions—and divides and fubdivides the ridiculous nothingnefs of his difcourfe —and forgets the beginning of his ftory, and wonders you cannot remember it— then paufes—hefitates—recollects, and begins again, the important narrative of fome family-connexion in the laft century—or the true and furprifing hiftory of his travels through London and Weftminfter.

He is but juft gone, as I hope you will imagine, by my fretfulnefs not having fubfided ; but indeed I had caufe to be angry, for he banifhed a train of very agreeable ideas, which are now irrecoverably loft.

I will therefore trouble you with no farther addition at prefent than my thanks

thanks for your remarks on Sterne, and the complimental allufion, deferring till my next, the catalogue of beauties in his Sentimental Journey.

To * *.

I HAVE heard of your coxcomb vifitor, and fee him very plainly in your defcription; but you need not have told me you were angry, for I could *read* that in the fpirit and volubility of your expreffion. Nothing more voluble than a lady's anger.————Enough of this, I have fomething elfe to communicate. You muft go to the play tomorrow. *Garrick performs.* Mrs. ***
has places, and will fend to you in the morning.

morning. ** is of the party. I fhall drop in by accident. Do not refufe. You can have no objection; and I hope have no pre-engagement.

To the fame.

I WAS aftonifhed this morning at hearing that you went away fo early. I thought at leaft you would have ftaid dinner, and wanted to make excufes for my *defertion* laft night. Shall I fay it was on your account? a bad *compliment* indeed, but I really fancied you feemed under reftraint. You were fo very filent, and the reft fo very talkative, that in fhort I grew tired; and after pleading

engage-

engagement, could not decently return.

Let me hope for a line to-morrow.
Were you well entertained? I thought
Garrick as great as ever. Adieu.

———————————

T *.

YES, my Lord, I was extremely
well entertained: but (pardon me
for returning your *compliment*) was much
happier after your departure; not merely on account of restraint, but had you
not withdrawn, I had lost one of the
highest pleasures a sensible mind can enjoy, which is, hearing the praises of
those it values. Some company that sat

near

near us, I don't know who they were,
but the moment you left the box they
began to fpeak of you . . . and . . No
. . . not one word fhall I repeat. I remember your caution, and will ever
" beware of flattery."   Sufficient for
me that I *heard* thefe praifes: they were
honeft and judicious, doing infinite credit to thofe who beftowed them, and
giving exquifite pleafure to your Friend.

To * *.

I THANK you very fincerely for the
generous intereft you took in thofe
people's difcourfe, and for the commu-
nication of it: not that either reflects fo
much honour upon me as upon your

own

own heart; but I regard the firſt as a proof of friendſhip, and the latter as a mark of confidence; and again thank you heartily for both.

There was a little error in the beginning of your letter—but excuſable, conſidering how late we converſed—I called at * yeſterday, and heard that you intended them a viſit on Monday. They expeɛt you to ſtay all the week. I ſhall have the pleaſure of ſeeing you perhaps once more, but not ſo often as I could wiſh. Adieu.

D   To

To *.

NOT having an opportunity (tho' I wifhed and fought for it) of fpeaking to you alone at Mr. *'s, I am obliged to this method of acquainting you with a circumftance on which I fhall prefume to claim your friendly advice.

It was not (as you know) till very lately that I could *properly* eftimate my own poffeffions of this world's goods. Small are thefe poffeffions, 'tis true; yet confiderable enough to occafion difpute, for which, and other reafons, I am making my *will*. It has employed me fome time, for I cannot pleafe myfelf in the difpofitions. I wifh to leave more

to

to charitable ufes than *fome people* would approve, whilft *others* would perhaps be as well pleafed with a ring as a legacy: now thefe laft ought in juftice to have the preference; and yet (but herein I difcover great weaknefs) I am hurt by the idea of leaving *any one* diffatisfied with my memory. I would alfo —but I fhall enclofe papers, in which my reafon for every thing will appear. Pray read them at your leifure, and favour me with your free opinion, which fhall be decifive.

I fear you will think there is too much of *trifling circumftance.* Be pleafed. to make fome allowance for *fex,* and then cenfure unfparingly whatever appears like vanity, fingularity, or affectation.

I do

I do not apologize for troubling you on this particular occafion; becaufe there is not a *difinterefted* perfon on earth that I can confult, excepting your ... felf.

To * *.

AT the firft glance of your requeft, recollecting your age and appearance, I was furprifed, and fhould have thought a marriage-fettlement a more proper fubject of advice; but you are perfectly right.

I fhall not keep you long in fufpenfe for my opinion, having devoted this whole day to the perufal and confideration

tion of your papers, and am determined to approve myſelf an honeſt
lawyer. I am charmed with ſome of
your diſpoſitions, and hope it will be
.... let me ſee .... juſt ſeventy-five
years before they take effect. Adieu.

T *.

" WHAT thanks ſufficient, or
what recompence equal, have
I to render?"

You do not require any—you forbid
all acknowledgments. So be it then.
The draught is executed; it was copied
verbatim; it ſatisfied all my doubts, and

D 3 will

will do me hereafter more credit than I deferve.

Pray my ..... I beg your pardon, but pray have you forgot affigning me a tafk (fome time ago) in the *Sentimental Journey?* I am now going to execute it, by telling you what parts of it I chiefly admire—— .

Firft then, the defcription and cha‑racter, and hiftory, and in fhort, every fyllable concerning Father Lorenzo. The Preface. The art of making love. The paffage at page 85, beginning " I pity the man." The diftribution of the eight fous. The character of Le Fleur. The dead Afs. The Bookfeller's Shop, and walk to the Rue de Guineygaude. The Starling. The Captive. Le Pa‑tiffier. The Sword. La Dimanche.

Maria.

Maria. The Bourbonnois. The Supper, and the Grace.

Thefe are all the chapters I *thoroughly* approve. There are others perhaps equally agreeable to. other taftes; and fome I fancy that very few can admire. I have wondered fometimes, as Mr. Sterne fhone fo much in the pathetic, that he never introduced the diftrefs of a tender mind on a recent lofs by death. Perhaps he might intend it, and was prevented *by* death from increafing that forrow which fome tender mind might feel for *his* lofs. " Alas, poor Yorick !" What an expreffive epitaph! He fairly appropriated it to himfelf. " There be no more fuch *Yoricks*."

To

To * *.

I HAVE not had a leifure moment
fince I faw you, or I fhould not fo
long have delayed afking your pardon
for that unwelcome vifit. Hear the
true ftate of the cafe, and believe me
when I *again* proteft it was entirely accidental, and very far from my intention.

I told you where we had been, and
upon what bufinefs. On paffing your
houfe, *** remarked it as a pretty box
which he had never obferved. Returning, he pulled the ftring in order to take
a nearer view; and declared it was in
good tafte. The miftrefs of it, faid I,
fmiling, is a particular friend of mine.
                                   That

That inftant, on the carriage ftopping, you came to the window. There's the lady, I fuppofe, faid ***; a fine wo-man, an *elegant* woman, by — ! Let us alight for a moment. Without waiting my anfwer, he opened the door himfelf; I followed him; you know the reft; but as we did not trouble you with *much* of our company, I will depend on your forgivenefs.

As for ***, he is enraptured with you. He afked a thoufand queftions; and even talked of making you another vifit; but I put him off this, and you need not fear it, for he fails in a few days. I don't remember whether that was mentioned in our fhort converfa-tion, but you obferved, I dare fay, how

D 5 *fatisfied*

satisfied he is with his new dignity. I want your opinion of him. You will give it me to-morrow. Adieu.

To *.

I SHALL not venture to give my opinion of any perfon at a time when I am difpleafed with them. You will excufe me from that tafk. Your *friend* —is he your friend?—was fo extraordinary civil as to make me another vifit this morning. Had I been aware of this honour, I would moft certainly have declined it. I am loth to tell you how much it difturbed me. More indeed than it ought ... but his ftrange introduction, his unpolite behaviour—I had

rather

rather he had owned his motive to be
ill-bred curiofity—but " a defire of rendering me fervice."—He " did not
know but I might have fome commands
abroad." Ridiculous!——We were fitting in awkward filence when the *diligence* came with your letter. I rang
to have it brought in; and detained the
fervant by a motion, as if I thought
*** was going. Upon this he arofe,
and very impertinently offered to look
at the *addreffe*. I concealed it; and out
of all patience at fomething he *then* faid,
told him I had the honour to wifh him
a good morning. He feemed furprifed
and difpleafed, but recollecting himfelf, made his compliments, and withdrew.

D 6   But

But how to account for this ſtrange behaviour;—and now that I have given you theſe particulars, it appears in a ſtill more diſagreeable light, and pains me exceedingly. I ſuppoſe he thought —I don't know what he thought——I believe you will ſcarcely be able to read this, it is ſo blotted by the tears which I cannot reſtrain . . . ... the tears of pride, anger, and vexation.

To * *.

THAT fellow's impertinent viſit did not give you more pain than your recital of it gave me. I am extremely concerned that any inadvertence of mine ſhould coſt you a tear. I hope

hope he did not prefume ..... pardon me, I mean not to trouble *you* with enquiries; but of this be affured, that had your letter arrived a few hours fooner ..... yet 'tis no matter, he has left England, and may perhaps never return. Dry your eyes, therefore, and think no more of an event which, after all, is not worth a *ferious* thought. Some ladies would have been very well pleafed with fuch a vifit, imputing it to their *irrefiftible* attractions. I will allow *you* to be *dif*pleafed; but I will not allow it a place in your memory.

You muft not be offended at my affuming this high privilege of controlling your thoughts. I am authorized by the' knowledge of your difpofition. Strange indeed, after three years ftudy and ob-

fervation

fervation on the book of your mind, if
I could not tranflate your ideas, in whatever language they are expreffed, with
tolerable precifion.

An inftance in point. Your *chapters*
of *Sterne* were all previoufly marked by
my pencil, as what I fancied you would
prefer. To fay truth, I had marked a
few more, and think ftill that you would
have mentioned them, but for reafons
which I can *as* eafily guefs.

See what knowledge I pretend to!
Expofe me, if I am *but* a pretender;
for there are too many of them in all
arts and fciences, not excepting this moft
difficult one of human nature.

Adieu.

Adieu. When and where shall I see you?

To *.

INTENDING myself the honour of seeing you very soon, I decline any particular answer to your last.

I must again have recourse to that friendship of which you have given so many generous proofs; and beseech your advice on a subject of some importance.

I intended to have decided for myself; but have not strength of mind to deter-

determine which of two alternatives *is right.*

From your judgment I will make no appeal, though it fhould be contrary to my wifhes, nor will I be partial in the evidence. Vouchfafe to hear and decide this caufe *to-morrow,* if poffible. I fhall wait on you about noon for that purpofe, and if you are abroad or engaged, fhall expeft to *hear* when it will be more fuitable.

A certain fortunate knight. (we are told in the volumes of romance) had an infallible guide or dirertor in a myfti-cal pyramid of adamant, on the fides of which there appeared every morning engraven, by an invifible agent, the actions he was to perform that day.

While

While I confult you thus frequently and have the benefit of your advice, *your friendſhip* is to me that pyramid, that guide, that ſteady and infallible director.

To * *.

I HAVE nothing to communicate, and write only to enforce my advice, which I hope you will *ſtrictly* follow. I am aſtoniſhed, that you could heſitate a moment, for, notwithſtanding the acknowledged gentleneſs of your temper, I am certain you prize your independence.

Were

Were parents *or* children in the cafe, it would be different, but in *your* circumstances, good God, what a ridiculous proposal!

Let no perfuasions affect you, haften your *tour*. That will fhew them you are and will be your own miftrefs. I wifh you health and a pleafant journey. Adieu! May your adamantine pyramid be an happy omen! May our friendfhip be as durable as permanent!

To *.

I HAVE had a very agreeable excurfion, and employ the firft moments of my return in writing to my noble

noble friend. What do I owe ... what
do I *not* owe to his counfel! I found,
after affuming a little refolution, that
nothing *elfe* was wanting to fatisfy all
parties.

Here then I pitch my tent, and here
I find almoft every requifite of happinefs. You remember thefe lines:

An elegant fufficiency, content,
Retirement, rural quiet, *friendfhip*, books,
Eafe, alternate labour, ufeful life,
Progreffive virtue, and approving heav'n.

I enjoy moft of thefe : let me practife, let me merit the reft!

I hear that you left town on Wed-
nefday: this letter therefore falutes you

at

at *. That charming, that envied retreat, where I fancy you enjoy yourfelf infinitely better than in London.
How many reafons there are for the
preference! 1 might perhaps regard *
with a partial, a prepoffeffed eye, for I
have never yet feen a place I like half
fo well. I remember walking through
its facred groves with a confcious, an
enthufiaftic pleafure, that, had I been
a favourite of the mufes, would certainly have burft forth into the raptures of
poefy.

I fhall think myfelf happy, (if it adds
to your fatisfaction) in the continuance
of this intercourfe by writing. The
fufpenfion, though fo fhort, has con-
vinced me how much I am interefted in
the renewal. You may depend too, upon

on never being troubled again with ridiculous apologies and excuses. You have cured me entirely of that foolish pride, which was hurt by corresponding with a fine writer. I am sensible that it would be difficult for you to *find* an *equal* correspondent, and I acknowledge, with gratitude, your readiness in stooping to those who are unable to rise to you. In fine, I have adopted your opinion, that familiar letters may, with propriety, be incorrect, or, in Mr. Pope's words, that " The Letters of Friends are not the worse for being fit for none else to read ;" and the certainty that none else *will* ever peruse my letters, has made me perfectly easy in that respect.

Enclosed

Enclofed I have taken the liberty to fend a few trifling remarks made by way of journal, during our little tour. They will inform you how my time has been fpent, fince I had laft the honour of fubfcribing myfelf your moft obedient.

To * *.

YOU muft indeed regard * with a partial eye if you prefer it to other places, when you are juft come from feeing feveral finer. I thank you for your ingenious and entertaining remarks; and will return them, prefuming, by the different writings, that you have no copy.

And

And are you really fo partial to * ?
Shall I put you to the teſt ? Come, and
pay it a viſit this ſummer. Here are
ſome alterations on which I ſhould like
your opinion. I expeſt Mr. and Mrs.
* * *; and ſhall be glad if their company, or any other inducement ſhould
draw you hither. Conſider of this invitation. Don't you · think in your
heart, that mankind would be happier,
if they ſacrificed more to friendſhip and
leſs to punſtilio.

You ſuppoſe that I enjoy myſelf better here than in town. I *do* in many
reſpeſts : but ſhall I own (it is without
repining) I am not ſuperlatively happy
any where. Once, indeed . . . .

Ah ! happy hours, beyond recovery fled,
What ſhare I now that can your loſs repay !

I never

I never arrive at this place without fome fuch thoughts as the above; and at times, in my folitary rambles, I find them ..... too deeply impreffed on my memory. Even at this inftant ..... but no more ...... You have an intelligent mind, and a feeling heart: You will comprehend my meaning, and perhaps add one generous tear to thofe which involuntarily drop from the eyes of your friend.

To

To *.

O the foft commerce! O the tender ties!
Clofe twifted with the fibres of the heart,
Which broke, break *them*, and make it pain
    to live!

I CANNOT tell you how many tears I fhed over the moft affecting lines that ever were written. I wept from fympathy, from too keen a fenfe of that forrow, which I hoped *you* had no longer felt. I thought *your* griefs had, by the flow and lenient hand of Time, been changed into a remembrance rather fweet than painful,

    Which footh'd with tend'rft thought your
       aching breaft,
    And built delight on woe.————

I am concerned to find it otherwife, and am at prefent in fo penfive a mood,

E   that

that I forefee this letter will be nothing
but a ſtring of melancholy reflections.
My breaſt harbours more griefs than
one, and it will be ſome relief, if you
ſuffer me to confeſs, that I ſtill mourn
inceſſantly a loſs to which the world believes me thoroughly reconciled, or
rather that it muſt have been wholly
abſorbed in one more recent.   How
are they miſtaken! I had two altars in
my heart.   The flame of conjugal affection never eclipſed that of the *filial*;
nor was the extinction of it more painful. A number of alleviating circumſtances . . . . . but this is not a ſubject
to be dwelt on.   I was only going to
obſerve, that no calamity can more
forcibly, more laſtingly, affect a perſon
of my diſpoſition, than the ſudden
death of a friend by whom we *knew* that

we

we were beloved. I have not been wholly exempt from other trials, and may therefore venture to form a judgment. The lofs of fortune, or indeed any difafter that affects one's felf alone, leaves many refources. There is a moderation to be fhewn which enables one calmly to bear the fuffering, or a noble firmnefs which raifes one above compaffion. The natural *vanity* of the human heart will fometimes confole us in adverfity. Self-admiration is often a powerful comforter, but wholly ineffectual againft the ftroke which lays one who loved us in the duft. We are then awed by humility. We call to mind the good qualities of the deceafed, which " brighten as they take their flight :" *our own* fhrink from the comparifon, and and we are ready to en-

quire

quire why we fhould be yet favoured
with an exiftence of which they are deprived. Again, though we put felfifhnefs out of the queftion, and the de-
light, never more to be known, which
their friendfhip afforded, yet ftill we
find caufes enough to juftify unceafing
regret. In the words of an admired
author, " We confider, with afflictive
anguifh, the pain we may unthinkingly
have given them, and now cannot al-
leviate; and the loffes we may have
caufed, and now cannot repair. We
recollect a thoufand endearments which
before glided off our minds without impreffion, a thoufand favours unrepaid, a
thoufand duties unperformed, and wifh,
vainly wifh for their return, not fo
much that we may receive, as that we

may

may beſtow happineſs, and recompenſe
that kindneſs which before we never
underſtood."

If we add to this the reflection, that
they were ſummoned from a ſtate of
being in which they were uſeful, and
in which they would gladly have continued longer, it increaſes our trouble
to its higheſt degree, ſince almoſt every
event, and even the moſt pleaſing
events, may revive their ideas, with all
the bitterneſs of compaſſionate grief.
The various charms of nature which
they no more muſt behold, ſeem to loſe
their luſtre; and every enjoyment, becauſe *they* cannot partake it, appears
inſipid.

E 3

In.

In fhort, I believe it very poffible for one to become fuch a prey to forrow, as to think it wrong to feek confolation. This however is not *my* cafe. I have juft been *feeking* confolation. Pardon me; for it has been at your expence!

To * *.

Something too much of this.

I SHALL not re-perufe your letter, and am forry that I gave you occafion to write it. How came you by fo much more fenfibility than is neceffary to your happinefs? You are a young woman, and, in all probability, may reckon upon many years of life. It is

not

not for *you* to talk of " unceafing re-
grets," nor to indulge a habit of melancholy that cannot be fhaken off.
You muft look *forward.* I will venture
to prognofticate that there are many
happy days in ftore for you, many
bright hours in referve. Beware how
you *willfully* obfcure them by unavailing
forrow.

If your vanity bore any proportion
to your attractions, I fhould reprefent
to you, that a melancholy air adds not
to *your* charms but rather eclipfes them.
I would fay to you, (with *Malvolio*)
" Thy fmiles become thee; therefore,
in my prefence, fmile always, dear now
my fweet, I pr'ythee." This is not
pleafantry, for you really look infinitely
handfomer for cheerfulnefs, and when

E 4   earneftly

carneſtly talking, or attentively liſten-
ing, your face ... illuminated with
ſmiles .... but I will not flatter; *too*
often have I ſeen this ſun-ſhine unſea-
ſonably overcaſt by the cloud of thought-
fulneſs.

Let me hear from you ſoon, and in
a more ſprightly ſtrain. Adieu.

To *.

I OBEY your obliging command of
writing *ſoon*, but as it is not juſt
now in my power to aſſume a *ſprightly
ſtrain*, this will be a very ſhort treſpaſs
on your patience.

I mean

I mean only to apologize for my neglect in not having acknowledged the
honour of your invitation to *. There
is no reason why I fhould be infenfible
of that favour, though, alas! there is,
at the fame time, *no reafon why I fhould
accept it.*

Another apology occurs to me this
moment (which I intended making before your prohibition of them); it is
for the frequent ufe of quotation. I am
very apt to exprefs myfelf in other
people's words, merely becaufe they
occur more readily, and feem better
than my own. I wifh to know your
opinion on this head; 'tis not enough
that you occafionally *practife* quotation:
the queftion is, whether you allow it in
E 5   a general;

a general, an unlimited degree to your correfpondent.

To * *.

I ALLOW to my fair correfpondent not only the free ufe of quotation, (which, in familiar writing requires no apology) but every advantage, every indulgence fhe can devife; and all too little for the fatisfaction her correfpondence affords.

Your letter which came yefterday, awakened me from a very pleafing meditation on the rife, progrefs, and prefent ftate of *our* friendfhip, in which I had concluded it was eftablifhed on

fo

ſo ſolid a baſis, that neither time or chance (one accident excepted) could ever deſtroy it; and thus I argued the matter:

Friendſhip between two perſons of the ſame ſex, though extremely eaſy to be formed, is liable to diſſolution by a thouſand accidents, from which ours is ſecure. Sometimes a difference in taſte, ſometimes too great a ſimilarity, ſometimes intereſt, and ſometimes love, will ~~unite~~ the ſacred knot. Friendſhip between thoſe of differing ſex, is harder to form and to preſerve. Put conſanguinity out of the queſtion, and where will you find your frinds? Single or married, old or young, if they are of equal age, their ſentiment is not friendſhip . . . . . it is either *too cold*, or *too hot*. .

E 6 . Again, .

Again, if their age differs confiderably, their taftes will, in general, be too oppofite. Will a young man feek for *animated pleafure* in matronly converfation? Can a matron be fuppofed to relifh the wild fallies of youth? The very idea of fuch a connexion is ridiculous; but if adopted in fome degree, only the *fex* of the parties exchanged, I hope it will not appear fo.

Let us fuppofe that on the ground of long acquaintance, a ftrict and more particular friendfhip is formed, between an old man tolerably free from the vices of *his* age, and a young lady ftill freer from the foibles of *her's*. We ought to fuppofe, that they are both difengaged from the conjugal tie, and their fentiments fhould be pretty much alike upon

all

all fubjects. We will allow the lady to
fancy herſelf in ſome reſpects inferior,
particularly in learning or knowledge ;
becauſe that ſuppoſition, adding weight
to the experience of a friend, will produce truſt, counſel, and reciprocal confidence, all which are a powerful ce-
ment to friendſhip : and we may ſuppoſe
alſo, that ſhe is enabled to diſcloſe her
thoughts freely upon all ſubjects, without the leaſt impropriety ; *he* being,
from the very nature of things, abſo-
lutely diſintereſted in her regard, and
incapable of any other ſentiment than
a lively generous eſteem, which can never diſturb the repoſe of either.

And now, pray what is your opinion
of ſuch a connexion ? Is it not well
formed for *duration ?* Yea verily, and
the

the rather for its being of a gentle and
placid kind, forming, as somebody has
said, " no higher expectations than human nature can answer," and confe-
quently free from the disquiets and jea-
lousies which too often extinguish *violent*
friendships and romantic love.

———————

I had not half done with my subject,
but am very unexpectedly interrupted,
and as unexpectedly coming suddenly
to town. I think to see Mrs. *** on
Friday afternoon ...... Need I say
more? .... I can have no other opportunity of seeing you. Adieu.

To

To the fame.

I CANNOT reſtore your letter of this morning, for I put it into the fire the moment I had read it; being loath to *remember* that *your* pen had ever given me diſturbance.

Think not that I condemn your *motive* for writing. Friendſhip will ſometimes be officious: pardon this expreſſion. I ſaw that you were concerned for me laſt night, but as the occaſion (though too well known) did not eſcape my lips, it is more remarkable, pardon me again, that you ſhould trouble yourſelf to ſo little purpoſe.

There

There are some kinds of sorrow that will not admit of consolation. To one who has received a wound that he knows to be incurable, (unless the *sovereign Physician* should pour in the wine and the oil) how troublesome are the applications of empirics, and how impatiently does he listen to their prescriptions! Pardon me yet again for this allusion; but indeed, my good friend, you are not qualified .... You remember what *Constance* says,

He speaks to me that never *had* . . . . .

Experience alone can qualify .... but I desire not any of my friends to be so qualified.   N O.   God is my witness, I do not wish even the party in question to know by *experience*.

.

How fharper than a ferpent's tooth . . . .

. . . . . . impoffible to proceed . . . .

As for your allufion to the parable
. . . . but I cannot fay any thing
about it.

You imagine, perhaps, that this particular inftance . . . . I cannot write
. . . . . why, why did you give me the
occafion ?

Two o'clock.

What a wretch am I! how fortunate,
that I did not fend away the above till
I had recovered my fenfes! It is but
this moment I recollect having defired
(as I led you down ftairs) that you *would*
write; that you *would* " minifter to a
mind difeafed."

Pardon

Pardon me now, once for all, my most amiable friend. I will not keep back my letter. I know you have magnanimity enough to excuse and pity me. Besides, I have an unhappy *additional* cause . . . .

With the strictest the most jealous secrecy have I hitherto preserved *this* hoard of sorrow; but I am now almost tempted to pour it, without reserve, into your friendly bosom, and seek the long lost charm of sympathy. I know not what to resolve . . . . I will meet *Dispatch* in his return, and if he tells me you are alone, I drink tea with you. But do not lead to the subject, I conjure you. Let the impulse of the moment determine whether it shall *ever* be disclosed. Adieu.

3

To

To the fame.

HOW unreafonable is your friend!
He expected to fee you but once,
he has already feen.you twice, and is
now pining with regret becaufe he cannot have a third interview. But what
is this urgent bufinefs that fends you
galloping away, and in a ftage-coach too,
of all vehicles, at the very inftant when
we ought to have met? I muft fet off
myfelf to-morrow .... I wifh I could
but contrive ... and why not?...Enough
... don't be furprifed.

" *I'll meet thee at Philippi.*"

To

To *.

I AM returned already, much fooner indeed than I expected : but what am I to fay my *humble friend!* You do not expect an acknowledgment? I fuppofe there hardly ever was fuch an inftance of .... I don't know what ... and yet believe me, I was more pained than obliged; but I hope you fuffered no inconvenience.

The *woman* unfolded herfelf at laft. She keeps a fhop at L. in W. and the *man*, as *fhe* told me, has a place in the navy-office. I wonder what .... but as Hamlet fays, " There is no wonder; or elfe all is wonder."

I expect

I expect the honour of a line from you very foon, and fhall be happy to hear that you are in perfect health.

———————————————————
———————————————————

To * *.

BE happy, for you have the honour to hear that I am in perfect health.

Serioufly, I am tolerably well; I got here in very good time, and moreover I have loft the cough, which was fo judicioufly pronounced to be *a troublefome companion.*

You fay nothing of your own health, but I flatter myfelf you are well. Your conftitution, though delicate, feems naturally

turally good. Be careful to cherifh a bleffing, without which you can relifh no other.

I have frequently wifhed, and more within thefe few days than ever, (ex-cufe this abrupt introduction) that you could *conveniently* make fome little alte-ration in your manner of living, and appear more in the world. You know my reafons for this wifh. Let me once again urge them to your confideration. Recollect alfo, what Mrs. *** faid to you concerning the " folly, fin, and danger of being righteous overmuch." It was once hinted to me, but not by *her*, nor do I enquire into the truth of it, that your annual expence in *charity* would keep you a *carriage*.

Now

Now I think .... but you know my thoughts already. A little more eclat, a little more folly and impertinence, a great deal more freedom and fatis-faction.

Adieu.

To *.

HAVING nothing at prefent worth communicating to my noble friend, I fhall only defire he will not credit an idle report, and then fubmit to his perufal

A FABLE.

Once upon a time a poor widowed linnet (who unfortunately loft her mate

in

in the barbarous *shooting-season,* and who was not inclined to seek another) found great difficulty in keeping the possession of her own solitary nest. She had moreover the ill-fortune to be entangled unawares in a *net,* which proved mostly fatal to birds of her size; for the smaller ones often crept through the meshes, while those of superior size and strength could break the net and escape. In this distress she applied to an eagle, that dwelt in the *forest* adjacent, by whom she was slightly known. This generous bird readily gave his assistance towards extricating her from the *net,* and afterwards continued to shew her great countenance and favour. Being unused to the conversation of linnets, he thought her rather more clever than the generality of that species, and even imagined

that

that fhe might prove an agreeable acquaintance.

Every one that knows any thing of
natural hiftory knows that birds, like
the human race, have many different
degrees or claffes of rank and prece-
dence. · The eagle, regardlefs of this,
continued to vifit the linnet, and in pro-
cefs of time, defirous of more *frequent
interviews*, became urgent with her to
remove into his neighbourhood, among
the birds of diftinction, alledging that
fhe was *extremely well qualified* to figure
in a higher fphere. The linnet knew
better, but at length, with infinite reluctance, fhe yielded to over-perfuafion,
and forfaking her peaceful thicket, was
introduced by the eagle to the beau-
monde of the feathered creation.

F   The

The novelty of the fcene engaged a little attention at firft; but foon, too foon, the grand miftake became vifible. The linnet *was not qualified.* She could not fing like the blackbird, fhe could not difplay the rich plumage of the goldfinch, fhe could not converfe with the deep-learned falcon, nor join in the mufic of the nightingale.

A thoufand beaks were now opened againft her, a thoufand reafons given for her fudden attempt at *politeffe,* and all equally unfavourable. She could fee the eagle, 'tis true, every day, but that was no comfort, for every day brought new proofs that fhe was no companion for *him.* He wifhed her a hundred times at that diftance, in which alone her merit appeared confpicuous; but the removal

was

was not without its difficulties. The birds whofe fociety fhe had left, were now equally prejudiced againft her, and fhe had neither fpirit nor intereft to make new friends. Alas for the poor linnet: difregarded by one party, difowned by the other, fhe expired with mere fhame and vexation; acquitting her benefactor, and condemning only her own folly!

To * *.

I AM delighted with your Fable; there is a fingular, a very *ftriking* ingenuity in the conftruction of it; but like other pieces of *ancient* writing, (for you know birds have not fpoke for fome ages) it is

liable

liable to divers readings, at the pleasure of different critics. I could propose two emendations, one respecting the *eagle* as you call it, but which according to *Le Pere* and *La Mere*, never classed so high, and, in fine, was but a *blackbird*; and if you consult that venerable and decisive critic, Father *Time*, you will find him give a different *catastrophe* to the fable; making the blackbird to die first, and to reproach the linnet with *not having accepted his proposal*, and rendered more happy that short time which his advanced age would allow him to expect in the forest of life. I shall not however attempt to influence *your* judgment by these remarks. Continue to read your fable just as you please.

But

But it will not be amifs to affure you, that I defire not a more frequent inter-courfe *merely* through felfifhnefs. I am vain enough to imagine that I could oc-cafionally add to *your* fatisfaction; for you have often very politely exprefied' pleafure in my' company, and feemed amufed by the anecdotes which my ac-quaintance with former times enabled' me to communicate. But I will not urge this matter farther, nor ever defire you to do any thing irreconcileable with' your own judgment. Adieu.

To.

To *.

YOU are infinitely obliging to drop a fubject on which I fhould be at a lofs to fay more. It is very certain that your converfation would at all times contribute to my improvement and hap-pinefs; and yet .... but what would I fay .... we have difmiffed the fubject.

I am not however provided with another; and muft confider a little be-fore I can determine upon what fpecies of nothingnefs to trouble you with.

Pray have you read *Emily Montague?* an important queftion, no doubt;—but I afk it only with a view to obtain your opinion of Mrs. *Brooke*'s writings in *general.* I cherifh a kind of vanity (and hope

hope it is not inexcufable) with regard
to the merit of my own fex ; and feel
gratified by every fuccefsful effort of female genius. You will laugh at my car-
rying this chimerical pride fo far ; but
I actually *triumph* in the notion that the
ftate of literature in England was never
more flourifhing than in the reigns of
Elizabeth and *Anne*.

I am not equally partial to the productions of modern writers of the other
fex; and have fometimes wondered to
hear *you* fo liberal in their commendations. But one reafon is, I am too apt
to compare them with their immediate
predeceffors, many of whom, beheld at
this favourable diftance, and advan-
taged by *your* accounts of them, feem

F 4   to

to me above all comparifon or imitation.

And pray, having mentioned comparifon, let me afk whether we have not
at prefent, *comparatively* fpeaking, *almoft*
as many good authors of the one fex as
of the other. *Brooke, Griffith, Macaulay, Carter, Montague, &c. &c.* The
characters of the two laft have been
long eftablifhed with me, becaufe they
have received the honourable ftamp of
your approbation. Upon the whole, do
we not ftand fome chance of fharing
your laurels?

To

To * *.

YES, I have read *Emily Montague*, and with a great deal of pleasure. Mrs. *Brooke* is a most ingenious woman. Her works are disgraced by the common appellation of novels. They are amiable and interesting pictures of life and manners, not absolutely perfect in resemblance, but sketched by the pencil of benevolence, and tinged with the delicate colouring of refined sentiment. Her descriptions of *Canada* in this work would do honour to an historian. She transports our imagination thither. We listen enraptured to the falls of *Montmorenci*.

Without answering your *comparative* question, I will allow that the ladies you name,

name, and a few others, feem likely enough to crop *fome* of our laurels. I wifh them all proper encouragement; but your fex is fufficiently formidable without the aid of letters; and the confequence might be dangerous if you encroached *too far* upon our province.

You fpeak of Mrs. *Macaulay.* She is a kind of prodigy. I revere her abilities. I cannot bear to hear her name *farcaftically* mentioned. I would have her tafte the exalted pleafure of univerfal applaufe. I would have ftatues erected to her memory; and once in every age I would wifh fuch a woman to appear, as a proof that genius is not confined to fex ... but ... at the fame time ... you'll pardon me, we want no more than *one* Mrs. *Macaulay.*

I do

I do not apologize to *you*, my fair friend, for this expreffion. It detracts nothing from female merit, and you muft allow that, generally fpeaking, each fex appears to moft advantage in the fphere particularly affigned it by Providence.

> For contemplation he, and valour form'd;
> For foftnefs fhe, and fweet attractive grace,

I come now to another part of your letter, and muft tell you, that I am not yet fo much of *an Old Man* as to refufe praife to all modern productions. We have authors now living whofe works will furvive them, and receive from the next age the applaufe which they folicit in vain from the prefent. That favourable diftance you fpeak of, and the dark veil of death caft over natural imperfections,

F 6

fections, are wonderful softeners of cri-
ticism, especially towards the productions of real genius, which can never
diminish in value.

Shakespeare is the most striking in-
stance of this truth. How gradual his
progress from neglect to admiration, to
reverence, almost to idolatry! But in
truth, (though no writer could *deserve*
more) he owes most of his fame to the
singular advantage of *a practical commen-
tator*, and must certainly be content to
divide *his* laurels with *Garrick*.

I have written enough at this time, or
I would mention some of our modern
writers whose works I like best, and their
several merits. I *shall* mention one,
though at the risk of offending you, by
remarking

remarking the capricioufnefs of your fex. 'Tis the author of *Sermons to Young Women*. You are indebted to this gentleman for two volumes of more elegant inftruction than has appeared fince the days of *Addifon*. He has held up to you a mirror ingenioufly conftructed and exquifitely polifhed, in which you may behold every feature of your minds, and improve them to the ftandard of perfection. At the firft publication of thefe fermons, recommended by novelty and fafhion, I met them in every houfe; I faw them upon every toilette. But where are they *now*; and how fell they into difgrace! Alas, they have been publifhed more than two years; they are become *antique*; they are loft, neglected, or forgot.

My

My letter is unreaſonably long, but,. ſpeaking of. modern merit, I cannot forbear telling you (though you will hear it ſooner perhaps by the news-paper). that *Powell* the player is dead. He will be very much lamented. A good actor is more generally miſſed than a good writer. I muſt own that I feel myſelf extremely concerned for his loſs. We can hardly forbear intereſting ourſelves about thoſe whoſe talents are publicly exhibited for our entertainment; while we are too often wholly indifferent to the more amiable characters of private life. Thouſands, like me, will acknowledge that they " could have better ſpared a better man;" and they ought as freely to acknowledge the ſelfiſhneſs of their motive. Poor Powell! He was rather a *pleaſing* than a *great* actor; but

he

he had not reached the fummit. That Theatre fuffers greatly. Your favourite, Mrs. *Arne*, was an irreparable lofs to it. I fhall never lofe the idea of that fweet little girl in fome particular charaĉters ... charaĉters fo well adapted to *her*, that I fhould not have patience to fee any body elfe *attempt* to play them.

And *you* will not have patience with *me* if I write fuch long letters; fo adieu.

T *.

YOUR refleĉtion on Mr. Powell's death, reminding me very forcibly of the brevity and uncertainty of human life,

life, brought on that penfive frame of mind which I am but too apt to indulge, wherein every amufement and purfuit of this tranfitory ftate appears beneath the regard of a rational being. I fay *too* apt to indulge, becaufe a *conftant remembrance* of thefe things might unfit us for the common offices of life, and detach us wholly from fociety.

Who that confiders the unfteadinefs of the foul and the frailty of the body, with the relation each bears to the other, that when the latter is afflicted by pain or ficknefs, the former is often a prey to fear and doubt; or that while the body appears found and healthy, the foul may make an *unprepared* exit; who that deeply confiders thefe things can avoid melancholy? Who, again, (fays

the

the moralift) that " confiders the limited
fpace of our exiftence, in comparifon
with eternity, but muft behold with
contempt the buftle that is made about
paffing this fhort period, and the various
aims and ambitions that are crowded into it ?" Our whole extent of being (con-
tinues he) is no more in the eye of *him*
who gave it, than a fcarce perceptible
moment of duration; and this refleftion
alone is fufficient to deftroy our attachment to the world, to render its gran-
deurs contemptible, and to make one
remain ftupified in a poife of inaftion,
void of all defigns, of all defires, of all
friendfhips.

It is well therefore for mankind that
they do not long retain thefe ideas, that
their paffions flow in and deftroy their
philofophy

philofophy .... but whither am I running, and why do I thus tire you with
trite and unconnected obfervations? I
will put an end to them and to my letter, for I know not how to enter upon
any other fubject: your literary remarks
would in a more cheerful hour have fuggefted many; but I can at prefent only
return my acknowledgments for them.

It occurs to me juft now, that I never
tranfcribed that fpeech from *Zingis*
which you requefted when I was com-
mending it; perhaps you have feen it
ere now; but my time is of little confequence; and it will help to fill up the
paper.

Ovifa

Ovisa contemplating the death of her Brother.

If e'er the spirit of a warrior slain
Journey'd in storms acrofs the troubled sky,
Laft night my brother *Zangon* pafs'd this place,
And call'd *Ovisa* home. The voice was deep
As when high *Arol*, shaking all his woods,
Speaks to the pafling thunder. Through my soul
A pleasing horror ran— ... Perhaps not long
Ovisa tarries here— ... The silent tomb
Is not the house of forrow.——Airy form
Of him who is no more! Where doft thou dwell?
Rejoiceft thou on golden skirted clouds?
Or is thy murmur in the hollow wind?
Where'er thou art, mine ear with awful joy
Shall liften to thy voice!—Defcend with night,
If thou muft shun the day. O ftray not far
From the remains of *Aunac*'s failing line!

I fancy you will difcover a great deal of *poetical* merit in this pafsage, and allow that it unites the fublime and beautiful.

To

To * *.

WITHOUT waiting your anfwer to my laſt, I write to congratulate you on your approaching nuptials. Mrs. *, who came hither laſt night, informs me that you are on the point of marriage with Mr. ****. I was *aſtoniſhed*; not at the event, for it is more furpriſing that you ſhould remain three years a widow; but I rather expeſted that you would have acquainted .... that is, I did not immediately confider how chary the ladies are of their love-fecrets; and indeed I had no right to expeſt ſo much confidence, therefore I beg you will not apologize on that account.

Mrs. * fays, you were at firſt averfe to the propofal; but the perfuafion of your

your friends; and the *amiable character* of your lover, has left no doubt of its fuccefs; in fine, that Mr. **** had told *her*, laſt week, that he would never re-linquiſh his pretenſions.

Strange indeed, if fuch gallant perfeverance did not carry its point. I muſt not venture to write again, leſt I fhould excite his jealouſy, and be miſtaken for a rival. But by his good leave, I will juſt call when I come to town, with my verbal compliments.

I fuppofe I fhall hardly know you again. 'Adieu now to grey luſtrings and plain linen! Welcome lace, jewels, and brocade! I muſt own I am impatient to fee this briſk youth, who has thus opportunely

Step'd

Step'd in with his receipt for making smiles,
And blanching sables into bridal bloom.

I hear he has a good estate, and is
" very much of the gentleman." There
was no doubt of your making a good
choice. I have only to repeat my congratulations, and wish you all possible
happiness, being very sincerely

Your Friend and humble Servant.

I only wait the receipt of your next
letter, to return .... it is this moment
put into my hands

————————

I have read it attentively; but disco-
ver no confirmation of the news. Let
me now see what I have been saying to
you on the supposition.———

How

How petulant! but I will not ſup-
preſs it. After all, I *am* a little hurt
by your want of confidence. Yet perhaps it is not true ... it ſeems unlikely
... you would not have wrote in ſo
grave a ſtyle ... Tell me ... but be
ingenuous ... Tell me the whole affair
.... It willl not diſturb *me* .... why
ſhould it ... I make myſelf ridiculous
... Pray do not keep me in ſuſpence.
Adieu.

To *.

UPON what circumſtances Mrs. *
founded her intelligence I cannot
poſſibly imagine, nor how ſhe came to
know ſo much more of the affair than
myſelf.

myfelf. Had I deliberated a fingle moment on Mr. ****'s propofal, I fhould
certainly have mentioned it to your
Lordfhip; and as it was, intended it,
the firft time I had the honour of feeing
you.

I don't know what he might fay to
Mrs. * laft week, but this week, at my
houfe, when I *repeated* a pofitive refufal of his fuit, he acquiefced in it like
a man of fenfe and a gentleman, com-
mending my plain dealing, and pro-
mifing never to renew a folicitation that
he faw was difagreeable.

He fet off yefterday for M—p—r with
his fifter, Lady **, who is ordered thither for the recovery of her health.

I have

I have never feen him above half a dozen times; and am forry even for thefe interviews, fince they have produced fuch an unpleafing confequence. I am *hurt* beyond meafure by your letter .... The manner of expreffion ... The fuppofition of my concealing fuch intelligence .... or that I could liften to offers of marriage. How little are my fentiments known to one whom I thought perfeɛtly acquainted with them! Married! and *you* to give credit!—*Married!* I fhould *indeed*

———— be dull of heart,
Taftelefs and grofs as earth, to think with patience,
Without abhorrence, of a fecond Hymen!"

I have never, 'tis true, made any formal declaration againft marriage, but on *this occafion* it becomes me to fay, that

G. the

the man lives not upon earth whofe name
I WOULD accept in exchange for that
with which I have the honour to fubfcribe myfelf your Lordfhip's moft obliged
and obedient humble Servant,

* . . . . **.

To * *.

*C*UPID and *Death,* fays the fabulift,
happening to fleep at one time in
the fame retreat, their *arrows,* being
fcattered on the floor, became intermingled; and each, by miftake, took
fome of the other's.   Hence the occafional mortality of *young* perfons, and
the dotage of *old* ones.

I was

I was fearful, t'other day, that the grim king of terrors, intending to cut my frail thread of exiftence, had only wounded me with a fhaft of *Cupid's*: fuch uneafy fenfations did the thoughts of your marriage occafion; but I was miftaken, and am glad to difcover, that my uneafinefs arofe folely from your fuppofed want of confidence.

You now, I think, feem to harbour *my* opinion of fecond marriages, but with lefs reafon. *You* might chance to marry happily, and I beg you, my dear child, to believe, that fuch a circum-ftance would give me infinite pleafure; that is, if you confulted me on it, and let me bufy myfelf about your fettle-ments, &c.

After

After all, I fear there is a little dif-
fimulation; and why fhould I diffemble?
... Adieu for the prefent; I am going
to walk .... and to *confider*.

———————

I have been re-perufing your letter,
my fair friend, under the fhade of a
fpreading oak, and there came to a refolution of entrufting you with my real
fentiments concerning it.

You have *voluntarily* difclaimed all
thoughts of changing your condition,
and I hope, therefore, that it is no breach
of friendfhip or delicacy to fay, that *I*
rejoice at it.

You muft not, however, enquire too
ftrictly after my *reafons* for faying fo;
they

they are fcarcely known to myfelf: for what fo deceitful as the heart?

The late Mr. * *, (of whom you muft undoubtedly have heard) upon a young lady's refufing his addreffes through favour of another, (who yet, for prudential reafons, was not much encouraged) prefented her with a handfome portion to enable her to marry that other. So at leaft goes the ftory, and I am ready enough to believe it, fancying that I could have acted juft in the fame manner. What greater confolation to a difappointed lover, than to render happy the object of his love, and awaken in her foul a tender and lively gratitude. And it might have gone farther; for had the lady's notions of honour borne any *refemblance* to thofe

of

of Prince Prettyman in the Rehearſal, ſhe would certainly have broke with the favoured lover, and married Mr. **.

If you ſhould aſk me now, why I have mentioned this anecdote, I ſhould be puzzled to anſwer you, for it bears no reſemblance to the affair in queſtion. Perhaps it was to obſerve, that the circumſtances being wholly different, I could not have made any merit to myſelf, nor received any recompenſe for the advantages I ſhould have loſt by your marriage. Do you aſk, what are theſe advantages? Your correſpondence; this familiar intercourſe, from which I derive a thouſand innocent pleaſures, and *that* place in your eſteem which I would fain *flatter* myſelf I poſ-   ſeſs, fefs, and which it is my *ambition* to preferve.

You will not mifinterpret what I have now written. I mean not to fhackle your affections, or vitiate your opinions. I defpife the ridiculous doctrine of Platonic love, and would no more be a Platonift than a libertine. All I contend for is the preference in friendfhip. You will allow there is fometimes a difference even in the *nature* of the fentiment. That which attaches me to you could not perhaps be eafily defined : nor is a definition neceffary. You may return it exactly in kind, without bewildering your fancy or endangering your peace.

G 4   Adieu.

Adieu. I pardon the formality of your fubfcription, having (very probably) given the example ... and I would apologize for the *ftyle* ... " *the manner of expreffion*" in my laſt ... but ... how can I be vain enough to imagine that it diſturbed you !

To *.

HAVING company who will prevent my writing by the Diligence to-morrow, I take the liberty of returning by Difpatch my fincere but haſty thanks for your moſt obliging favour.

I am flattered extremely by your generous profeffions of regard, and equally delighted

delighted with your approbation of my conduct, or more properly fpeaking, with your acquitting me from the change of levity in fentiment.

It will ever be *my* " ambition" to deferve *your* good opinion; having long adopted this maxim of an indifputable judge, that " *The thoughts of wife men are the true meafures of glory.*"

To *.

I AM to thank you for a piece of flattery fo very delicate, that I could not avoid reading it with pride and pleafure. Thefe elegant compliments, " where more is meant than meets the ear,"

ear," are of all others, moſt inſinuating. I never expeɛted that ſentence to be ſo applied.

But do you know that I am coming to town again? You will know it very ſoon; for I ſhall make you one of my firſt viſits, and to ſave the trouble of *introducing* the ſubjeɛt, will acquaint you before-hand with my principal errand. I am under the neceſſity of altering ſome diſpoſitions of my effeɛts, and intending to bequeath you a ſmall token of my ſincere regard, I would chuſe to do it in the manner moſt agreeable to yourſelf. Nor let your delicacy be hurt by the idea of this legacy. Remember you will not receive it till a time when the *diſintereſtedneſs* of the motive

motive will appear; but as Heaven only
knows how near that time may be, it
behoves me not to delay my intention.
Adieu.

To the fame.

" THE firft wrote, wine is the
ftrongeft; the fecond wrote, the
king is ftrongeft, the third wrote, women are ftrongeft."————

The third was in the right: neither
wine or the king would have been ftrong
enough to have altered my refolution,
but I fubmit to my *female* conqueror.

Yet

Yet obferve, that in this acquiefcence with your pleafure, I am (like our general parent)

——————————————Not convinc'd,
But fondly overcome by female charm.

I yield not to the ftrength of your reafoning, but to the force of your perfuafion, and now that I no longer *hear* you, am wifhing to renew my intention.

Let this, however, reft at prefent; for there is another thing that *muft* be mentioned. I had not courage enough for it yefterday ... do not be offended. To-morrow, about noon, a carriage will ftop at your door. It is your's. Your arms are on it. It was built for you. You cannot refufe it. The horfes are the colour you approve. They were

bought

bought on purpofe. I cannot endure
your going about in ftage-coaches. Pardon this foible in your friend, and make
him happy by accepting his prefent.

To *.

I HAVE fent for Difpatch to bring
you this, for I cannot wait the Diligence. Recall your orders, I entreat
you. Let it not come. I will not accept; I will not fee it. Cruel obligation. Diftreffing generofity. What return ... What acknowledgment ? How
could you *imagine* I would receive fuch
a prefent ? I need it not. I don't go
about in ftage-coaches. I have a chaife

to

to come to town, and when there, find
a chair more convenient.

I fhall be at *** this evening. If
you fhould chance to look in, let me
read in your eyes the forgivenefs of this
pofitive refufal, and a benevolent con-
cern for having given fo much pain to
my fenfibility. If you cannot come,
deign to call on me at * either Thurf-
day, Friday, or Saturday morning, to
receive my humble apologies and moft
grateful acknowledgments.

To

To * *.

I LEFT you very reluctantly yefterday, and had you *invited* me to dinner, fhould have broke my *engagement*.
We had a mighty infipid feaft. I went
home very early, and ruminated all the
evening upon your verfes. But my memory is bad. Pofitively you muft oblige
me with another fight of them. Without ocular demonftration, I would not
believe that you or any body could write
fuch an extempore.

I have ordered Difpatch to bring you
a coach and horfes. Now don't be a-
larmed again. 'Tis not for you, but
your little vifitor. I hope fhe will not
mortify

mortify me by the refufal of *a toy*
. . . . . . *you* have done that effectually.

I am not in good fpirits to-day.
The air feems *grofs* to me and heavy.
I have not, for fome years, breathed
freely in London, at leaft I fancy fo,
and intend to decamp very foon, I wifh
you could let me know when it will
fuit you to receive a tedious vifit. I
muft drink tea and fup with you. Be
alone; it is uncertain *when* we fhall meet
again. Adieu.

To

To *.

IF I am to fix a time for receiving the honour of your vifit, let it be Wed-nefday next. You will let me know whe-ther that day is fuitable ; but *I* fhall cer-tainly be difengaged, and I think too, you will then have the advantage of re-turning by the light of a *full moon*.

You had charmed my little gueft by your condefcending notice, and have now won her heart by your prefent. " She would give all the world, ay *twenty* worlds if fhe had them, to fee you again, and thank you for it, and fit on your knee, and fing you another fong." 'Tis an amiable little creature, and knowing enough for her age. " What a fine coach !" faid fhe; " O Ma'am, if it was

but

but a *little* bigger, and the horfes alive !"
Why what then ? " O then I'd get into
it, and fay, Here you Mr. Coachman,
carry me to the place you come from.
" I wonder," purfued fhe archly, " I
wonder where he would carry me to ?"
I can't tell really, but to the toy-fhcp per-
haps. She looked grave. " Ay, very
likely, but I don't want to go *there.*"

Need I apologize for this childifh
prattle ? Will you not rather efteem it,
as a pleafing proof that the human heart
is *very early* fufceptible of gratitude.

To

To * *.

I SWEAR to you my amiable friend, that I have not, thefe twenty years, enjoyed fo many happy hours fuccef-fively, as I did laft night in your company.

The variety of entertainment you provided, the elegant tranquillity of the fcene, the harmony of the invifible concert, the fimplicity of the repaft, the charms of your converfation ... I never faw you fo fprightly, fo animated .... Ah my fair friend! provide me no more fuch banquets ... I fhould pur-chafe them too dear.

What an odd compliment it is, to tell you I had a moft agreeable ride home;

home; I ought rather to fay, I left you and happinefs together; but it was no fuch thing; for the ferenity of the air, the brightnefs of the moon, and the ftrength of fome very pleafing ideas, infpired me with fo much chearfulnefs, that I perceived not the length of the way, and was even forry to quit my reverie.

But how will you excufe yourfelf for making fuch a rake of me? and how long do you think it is, fince I loft a whole night's reft? Are thefe frolics fuited to *my* time of life? You will fay I might have gone to bed this morning. That's true; but the rifing fun would have reproached me; and moreover—but your pardon . . . befides, *one* reafon is fufficient.

My

My dear Mrs. * *, I fhall efteem it a very particular favour, if you will immediately fit down, and acquaint me how *you* employ yourfelf, and what were *your* meditations, from the moment I left you till breakfaft time. *Mine* are committed to paper, and if you defire it fhall accompany my next letter.

I muft alfo requeft copies of your garden-infcriptions. I know they are from Shenftone and Akenfide, but I want to compare the alterations at my leifure.

Adieu. Accept a thoufand acknowledgments, and haften your anfwer.

To

To *.

IF I did not comply with your request *immediately*, I should most probably decline it; but am just now so pleased and flattered by your obliging compliments, that I cannot dispute your commands.

The moment, then, that your carriage was out of sight, I retired to my chamber, and as soon as all around me was quiet, I threw up the sashes for air, and began to walk very gravely backwards and forwards, endeavouring to recollect every circumstance of the evening, in order to censure or acquit my own behaviour and conversation. But this was not a very easy task; for the

Domestic

Domeſtic Deity, as Sterne moſt elegantly phraſes it, " was either talking or *pur-ſuing*, or was *in a journey*, or peradventure he ſlept, and could not be awoke."

So I ſat me down by the window, and watched the progreſs of the moon, who now,

Apparent Queen, unveil'd her peerleſs light
And o'er the earth her ſilver mantle threw.

Immediately ſeveral images of the poets, relative to this beautiful luminary, crowded into my thoughts; but I have more charity than to load you with the quotations.

I then imagined to myſelf, how far you were got by that time, and fancied that you (and perhaps numbers beſides) were

were *juſt then* contemplating and enjoy-
ing the mild luſtre of Cynthia.

> The conſcious moon, in every diſtant age,
> Hath held a lamp to wiſdom.——

Theſe meditations at length brought
on a ſuitable diſpoſition for Reflection
to aſſume the *cenſorial dignity*; and it
was aſſumed. The trial laſted near an
hour, when, after a full hearing, the
defendant was acquitted of capital impropriety, but convicted of ſome trivial
miſdemeanors, as too great a ſolicitude
to pleaſe, a little affectation, more vanity, and a large ſhare of ſimple credu-
lity. She was alſo indicted for having
received too much ſatisfaction; but
pleaded in excuſe, her intention of future ſelf-denial: upon which the court
broke up, without adjudging any *other*
puniſhment.

Now

· Now morn, her rofy fteps i'th' eaftern clime,
Advanc'd.

I was not inclined to fleep, and
fcarcely knowing how to employ myfelf, I went foftly down ftairs, and took
a few turns in the garden. Paffing by
the grotto, I chanced to efpy on the
table fome flowers that you had ga-
thered. They looked faded, but I
thought that water and a little attention
might revive them; fo I returned with
them to my chamber, and prefently after, addreffing myfelf to fleep, had a
comfortable repofe of two hours before
I arofe to breakfaft.

Here ends my journal, which I will
fend to you without reading it, left I

H   fhould

fhould repent of its unneceffary frank-nefs. Let me add, that the flowers being quite revived, I have difpofed them in a groupe, and am painting their portraits in water-colours, with this motto,

Live a little longer.

You defire copies of my infcriptions. I ought to mention, that the *tablets* are moveable, and very rarely exhibited; for the generality of my vifitors have no notion of fuch things, and would make them a matter of *wonderment.*

This is the firft :

O ye, who bathe in courtly blifs,
 Or toil in fortune's giddy fphere,
Do not too rafhly judge amifs
 Of one who lives contented here.

       Nor

'Nor yet difdain the narrow bounds
   That fkirt this garden's fimple pride,
Nor yet deride the fcanty mounds
   That fence yon waters peaceful tide.

The tenant of the fhade forgive,
   For wand'ring at the clofe of day,
With joy to fee the flow'rets live,
   And hear the linnet's temp'rate lay.

And O remember, that from ftrife,
   From fraudful hate. and frantic glee,
From every fault of polifh'd life,
   Thefe ruftic fcenes are haply free.

The fecond bears the alterations better; as you fhall judge. Indeed the
grotto was made to the infcription, and
not *that* to the grotto.

To me, whom in their lays, the fhepherds call
Felicia, daughter of content and health,
This cave belongs.—The fig-tree and the vine,

Which

Which o'er the rocky entrance downward fhoot,
Exclude the beams of Phœbus.—Cowflips pale,
Primrofe, and purple lychnis deck the green
Before my threfhold; and my fhelving walls
The honeyfuckle covers.   Here at noon,
Lull'd by the murmur of my rifing fount,
I flumber.—Here my cluft'ring fruits I tend,
Or from the humid flow'rs, at break of day,
Frefh garlands weave, and chafe from all my bounds
Each thing impure or noxious.—Enter in,
O ftranger, undifmay'd! and if a friend
To virtue, not unwelcome fhalt thou tread
My quiet manfion; chiefly if thy name
Wife Pallas and th' immortal mufes own.

I finifh this tedious lettter, having
nothing further to add or " *defire*," only
that you will pleafe to believe me, with
the moft refpeɛtful attachment,

&c. &c.

To

To * *.

AND so you have no curiosity—at least you do not " *desire*"——it's very well; and you certainly are—No —I will not compliment you at the expence of your sex.

I will not oppress you with compliments of *any* kind; but I thank you for the little narrative, and am charmed beyond expression by your amiable franknefs.

As for your *flower-piece*, (what an interesting, what an elegant thought!) remember that *I* befpeak it. You fhall not refufe it me; I will keep it for ever as a pledge of your generous regard.

H 3   I am

I am going out of town this very afternoon, to which I feel a fecret reluctance that makes it more neceffary.

" Il y a quelque fois dans le cours de
la vie de fi doux plaifirs, & de fi tendres
engagemens, que l'on nous défend qu'il
eft naturel de defirer du moins qu'ils
fuffent permis : de fi grands charmes ne
peuvent être furpaffés que par celui de
favoir y renoncer par vertu."

Adieu, ma belle veuve, vous étes
trop aimable !

To the fame.

I SHALL not fet out till to-morrow, and have two reafons for writing to you again.

I recollect fome expreffions in my letter this morning, that I fear will dif-pleafe you. I ftumbled upon them un-awares, but they exprefs *too much*, and almoft imply the exiftence of a fenti-ment, wholly unbecoming my age, and your character. We fomehow contract and retain a habit of what is called gal-lantry in fpeech; but 'tis ridiculous.— My good friend; I do *not* think you too amiable; I am abfolutely difiinterefted in your regard; nor can I be painfully or *improperly* affected by the united force of beauty, merit, and kindnefs.

You need not trouble yourfelf to anfwer this; I fhall write again the moment I arrive. Only be fo good to return the *inclofed*. It's the little picture you gave me fo long ago. I have had the drapery altered, and though prefume on your approbation, was willing you fhould fee it before the artift is paid. Adieu.

To the fame.

I AM arrived, and am tolerably well; but have very little elfe to fay to you. The *effential* in a letter of friend-

fhip

ſhip may generally be comprized in very few words. I intend ſoon to give you a ſpecimen (not a pattern) of bre-vity in writing, at preſent *I have not time.*

In our laſt converſation but one, you were obſerving, (and perhaps by way of reproach) that I never wrote to you *like a writer:* that if by great chance we entered upon a ſubject of importance, either moral or literary, I never treated it in a ſerious or argumentative man-ner. All this is very true; and yet I have been far from thinking my fair correſpondent

> ————Not with ſuch diſcourſe
> Delight; or not capable her ear
> Of what was high;————

But

But I have feveral correfpondences of the head, and wanted one of the heart. I find fo much pleafure in this indolent chit-chat, the fpirit of which would wholly evaporate in improvement, that I wifh to confine it to the moft familiar fubjects, or, more properly fpeaking, not to confine it at all; for the leaft degree of reftraint would produce delay, difguft, difcontinuance.—You have more than once charged yourfelf with imitating my ftyle; but, with fubmiffion, it is juft the reverfe; for I often catch myfelf adopting your's; nor did I ever before this intercourfe admire what may now be called *our* manner of writing; becaufe it leaves the *meaning* too often wholly dependent on the genius or fenfibility of the reader.

And

And now to convince you of my defire to oblige you in *all* refpects, I inclofe a manufcript for your more ferious perufal, your opinion, your ftrict
and unfparing criticifm. You will pleafe
to return it by the Diligence on Sun-
day, with as many obfervations on it as
fhall occur, and at the fame time, pray
favour me with a complete and *exact*
catalogue of your *library*. This is a
mighty whimfical requeft; but I want
much to know your favourite authors.
Adieu.

To

To *.

I AM infinitely obliged to you for this
  laft favour, and return the manufcript
with my obfervations and the requefted
catalogue, all which have taken fo much
time, that I can only juft tranfcribe a
few hafty lines, written yefterday, and
entreat you to let them pafs without one
fingle word of cenfure or commenda-
tion.   They are beneath criticifm.

The polifh'd labour of this heav'n-taught mind
    See the fam'd *Atticus* to *Mira* fend,
    And bid her freely cenfure or commend
What his creative genius has defign'd !

And though unfkill'd in fcience' mazy writ,
    She all unequal to the tafk be found ;
    And though the work be with perfection crown'd
By wifdom, learning, elegance, and wit.

Yet

Yet not in vain he makes the gen'rous loan,
   And not in vain the pleafing tafk requires,
Which gives her honour, leffens not his own,
   And her wrapt breaft with gratitude infpires:
So potent Phœbus bids the queen of night
Shine in the borrow'd beams of his reflected light.

To * *.

WELL, then, I will not praife your little fonnet, though it is *really* deferving; but I may thank you for the *obfervations*, which are extremely ingenious and valuable. If the work fhould ever *appear* (but that is unlikely) you would fee how much I regard them.

But why fhould you entreat me to let your verfes pafs without notice. In my opinion

opinion they are *not* below criticifm,. and I am in a criticifing humour; yet 'tis the lefs neceffary for me to indulge it with regard to this little piece, be-caufe your own judgment in thefe matters is exceedingly good, and I durft fay you know the *exact* degree of its merit.

It is one thing to tafte the perfection of an art, and another to excel *in* that art, but you might eafily unite thefe attainments; and although I do not think poetry your *forte*, nor would advife you to employ much *labour* in cultivating the laurels of Parnaffus, yet now and then an occafional effay will be an agreeable amufement not only to yourfelf, but to as many as you fhall think proper

to

to oblige with a fight of your performances.

Adieu. Simply adieu; for I know not what epithet to falute you with. I may fay to you in the *very* words of Queen Elizabeth to the bifhop's wife, " *Miftrefs* I *will* not call you, and *Ma-Dame* I *muft* not call you." More's the pity! Adieu. Pray obferve and admire this quotation, for it is the beft I ever made in my life.

To the fame.

HAVE you a mind to hear a very ridiculous inftance of the moft trifling vanity?

I was

I was fo pleafed with the fudden re-collection, and *the aptnefs* of Queen Elizabeth's faying, that I fent away my letter this morning without its principal errand, which was to invite you to dine with us at * to-morrow fe'nnight. I am not yet certain whether I fhall be at *the Jubilee*; but in either cafe fhall keep the above appointment, as it will be convenient in returning, and agreeable if I do *not* go, to meet thofe who have been there, and catch all their various reports before they circulate farther. Come therefore if you can; Mrs. *** will attend you; fhe talks of a party; I know you will not have the heart to refufe *her?* and filence fhall give con-fent. But why filence?—Why, becaufe I am compofing *another letter*, which you muft anfwer before we meet; and which

which will require a good deal of time and attention. The fubject is of fome confequence. I think to divide it into three feveral parts or fections, and would have you do the fame by your reply, in order to preferve that clearnefs or perfpecuity which ought to diftinguifh performances of this nature from effays of lefs importance. In a word, I am difpofed to make a full proof of your literary abilities. Go then, ftudy philofophy, and prepare yourfelf to anfwer the challenge.

To

To the fame.

ETES vous bien?
Je vous aime.
Dieu vous beniffe.

The Anfwer.

OUI.
Je vous remercie:
Et le bon Dieu vous beniffe encore.

To

To * *.

YOU will rejoice at finding your ftray fheep fafely inclofed in the fold of this letter; nor muft you be angry with your friends. I told you very truly, that I had not feen it; and Mrs. ***, with equal veracity, protefted that fhe had not got it; but we played the fable of the two thieves upon you; for fhe put it (unknown to me) into my pocket, and did not tell me of it till we were coming away.

I cannot however perfuade myfelf to prolong your uneafinefs, and have there-fore returned it at this unfeafonable hour, (and after *one* reading only) de-pending upon *your honour* for a fecond perufal.

perufal. It *muſt* be finiſh'd, indeed it muſt. Mrs. *** declares that you were no longer about it than whilſt ſhe was dreſſing. Indeed, my friend, you are .... but I durſt not ſay what. I durſt not ſay any thing more.

Good night! " *a thouſand times good night !*"

———

Daughters of *Britannia*'s iſle,
   Of ev'ry age and each degree,
Leave your native plains awhile,
   And haſte to *Shakeſpeare*'s Jubilee.

O gather ev'ry beauteous flow'r,
   And roſes fair with laurels twine,
And rob each fragrant myrtle bow'r,
   To deck your poet's hallow'd ſhrine.

And

And let no gentle voice be mute
 In the full chorus of his praife,
And let the fweetly founding lute
 Your foft harmonious concert raife.

But firft, arrang'd in decent throng,
 Repofe on *Avon's* verdant fide,
(How oft to hear the poet's fong
 Aas *Avon* ftopp'd his cryftal tide!)

Repofe, and liften to my lays ;
 Trembling, I feize the vocal fhell,
And in *peculiar* ftrains of praife
 Your *Shakefpeare's* merits aim to tell.

Let heroes fing his warlike pow'rs,
 Let kings his regal talents own,
Let poets, patriots, lovers - - - -

 - - - - - - - - - - -

Far diff'rent theme - - - - - -
 I fing the man, of tafte refin'd,
Whom wife unerring nature made,
 The judge, the friend of *woman kind*.

       O mafter

O mafter of the female heart,
    To whom its ev'ry fpring was known,
What rapt'rous joy didft thou impart
    To thofe who once poffefs'd thine own.

How bleft her lot, how envied now !
    Who clafp'd in thee a darling heir,
Or fhar'd thy tender plighted vow,
    Or claim'd thy fond paternal care.

Ye virgins, pluck the frefheft bays,
    Ye matrons, deck his honour'd bier,
Ye mothers, teach your fons his praife,
    Ye widows, drop the filent tear.

Now fpread the immortal volumes wide,
    And mark - - - - - - - -
- - - - - - - - - -
    - - - - - - -. - - -

No female guilt deforms the fcene,
    No female plots of terror rife,
Save where he fhews the murth'rous Queen
    Stain'd with ambition's *manly* vice.

                                        E'en

E'en while he acts *th' hiftorian*'s part
 He fmooths unnat'ral Regan's brow,
And foftens Cleopatra's art,
 And faithlefs Creffid's broken vow.

Nor partial fact -   -   -   -   -
 -   -   -   -   -   -   -   -   -
-   -   -   -   -   -   -   -   -   -
 Behold the lovely train appear.

With innocence Miranda charms;
 With virgin honour, Ifabel;
The filial heart Cordelia warms,
 And Portia's praife let *Wifdom* tell.

Bright fhines the hymenæal flame
 When Imogen's diftrefs is paft,
And vindicated Hero's fame,
 And Helen's patience crown'd at laft.

Thus diff'rent ftates are mov'd by turns;
 E'en aged hearts for Cath'rine glow;
And when diftracted Conftance mourns,
 Maternal bofoms throb with woe.

                                        But

But where, O Mufe, can ftrains be found
　　T' exprefs each virtue, charm, and grace
With which benignant *Shakefpeare* crown'd
　　The female mind, the female face?

Let me reftrain my grateful tongue,
　　And the exhauftlefs fubject quit;
Let Celia's truth remain unfung,
　　And Rofalinda's fprightly wit.

More tragic fcenes I now relate,
　　And tears of foft compaffion crave;
O pity Defdemona's fate!
　　O weep on poor Ophelia's grave!

And check not yet the tender tear,
　　Nor *yet* the rifing grief reftrain?
O'er haplefs Juliet's early bier,
　　Still let it flow, nor flow in vain.

When virtuous forrow prompts the figh,
　　And fwells the gen'rous feeling heart,
She adds to ev'ry glift'ning eye,
　　A charm beyond the reach of art.

? - - - - - - - - - - -
- - - - - - - - - - - -
- - - - - - - - - - - •
- - - - - - - - - - -

Cetera defunt.

To * *.

I DID not get home till very late laſt
night, and was extremely fatigued.

Parties of pleaſure are in my opinion
the moſt unpleaſant things in the world.
Indeed, nothing can be agreeable to me
that requires the leaſt activity, unleſs
it be in ſome degree intereſting; and
whenever I am buſying myſelf to no
I   purpoſe,

purpofe, I think on the labour of *the Danaides*.

The oftener I look on your *flower-piece*, the more I am charmed with it. Mr. * has pronounced it *beautiful*; and yet (fo capricious is my tafte) I have been chufing a place for it this morn-ing, where fcarcely any body will fee it but myfelf.

Have you feen your books? Do you like them? They were to be fent du-ring your abfence. Now you know why I requefted a catalogue; that I might not order any you had. Your library was too fmall; and if you fcruple to accept this trivial addition, I fhall fcruple to call you my friend, or fub-fcribe myfelf your s.

To

T *.

YOUR menace, my generous friend, has its effect. I dare not *scruple* to acept your prefent. But could I have divined your reafon for inquiring after my books, I fhould certainly not have fent the catalogue. As it is—if I muft fubmit—if you will not allow me to re-turn a few of the moft coftly, particu-larly the Natural Hiftory, I muft endea-vour to be eafy—as eafy as a mind not ungenerous can be under an oppreffive weight of obligation.

I think, if I know my own heart, it is in thefe inftances above affectation; nor is it deftitute of fenfibility . . . . . I need not explain what you very well un-derftand . . . *May I return any of the books?*

I 2 To

To * *.

I AM afraid, by the ftyle of your's, that my laft letter was *too authoritative.* I remember being in an ill-humour, but furely it extended not to you, nor could you mifinterpret the *menace.*

I know very well that you have lefs affectation and more fenfibility than half your fex; but have you not alfo rather too much punctilio? ... Return the books! Return the Natural Hiftory! which, of all others, I marked out for your particular amufement, having heard you in a manner wifh for it. You muft *not* return any of the books, nor muft you be uneafy at accepting them. You would not, if you were thoroughly acquainted with the difpofition of the giver:

for

for I think if (in your language) " I know my own heart," it feels for you all the *beſt parts* of the ſentiments which form the different charaĉters of a father, a brother, a guardian, and a lover. Are not theſe affeĉtion without authority, eſteem without jealouſy, watchfulneſs without intereſt, and tenderneſs without deſire? .... But perhaps you do not like theſe *abſtraĉted* notions, nor will, upon ſuch terms, acknowledge yourſelf my daughter, ſiſter, ward, or miſtreſs. Continue then, my *friend*, and believe that I ſhall ever be your's.

To

To *.

FINDING myfelf in a fcribbling mood, I am going to write without waiting to hear from you, but fhall not fend away my letter till I have that pleafure.

I cannot *juft now* recollect *who it was* that one of his friends complimented by faying, that " his entertainments pleafed not only at the time he gave them, but the day after." I fhould have liked vaftly to have been a gueft at fome of thefe entertainments, for I am not fortunate enough to find many that pleafe at the time, much lefs in recollection. I am juft returned from a vifit, and have left a circle of company, all polite and accomplifhed, all in *Smirk*'s words, fine

in

in figure, high in tafte, *tout magnifique & galant.* I have left this circle without pleafure or improvement, and reckon the time loft that I fpent in it; yet was in good fpirits all the while, and as talkative as any prefent.

And now you will expect me to give a reafon for my diffatisfaction. Believe me, it is not that I think myfelf wifer or better than other people, nor am I juft now unqualified for *polite conver-fation*; my late attendance on Mrs. *** having enabled me to give my required opinion on *moft* of the fafhionable topics.

But I mean to obferve, that however well fuch kind of difcourfe may beguile the prefent moment (and it will not do

I 4

that unenlivened by remark and repartee) it leaves no agreeable traces behind. It refembles " a fwiftly paffing cloud, on which fome faint beams of light have imprinted their weak and tranfient colours;" while the animated converfations of real friendfhip remain faftened on the mind, and as the wife Man faid of words that were fitly fpoken, are like " apples of gold in pictures of filver." In fine, my peculiar difpofition is fuch as would induce me (with Mr. Pope,) to value one tender well-meant word, above all that ever made me laugh in my life."

Interrupted.——Your letter.——— What fhall I fay to it? O my beneficent friend, you may guefs its effects on
the

the temper I have fo artlefsly confeffed.
Yes, I will accept your prefent, I will
efteem—I will acknowledge .... but
whither does my fenfibility tranfport me?
Allow me to break off————

Afhamed of the inequalities in my
own mind, I have often endeavoured
to difcover the fame failing in others;
and of all perfons upon earth, I am the
moft apt to compare myfelf with *Rouffeau*. We certainly do refemble each
other. I was very defirous of feeing
him on that account, and regret that I
did not. I can allow for all the pecu-
liarities that fo ftrongly mark his character. Like him I cannot avoid being
fretful, haughty, uneafy, difturbed even
by the fhadow of an obligation; yet
place the fame circumftance in a diffe-

I 5   rent

rent light, it foftens me into conde-
fcenfion, and overcomes me with joy.
People of this very fufceptible caft have
a thoufand pleafures and uneafineffes
of which others have no idea; but the
latter too generally predominate, and
verify thefe elegant and often-quoted
lines:

> Nor peace nor eafe the heart can know,
>> Which like the needle true,
> Turns at the touch of joy or woe,
>> But turning, trembles too.

But the principal inconveniencies of
ftrong fenfibility are the abfurdities of
conduct it gives rife to, which though
involuntary at the moment, are foon
keenly felt, and feverely repented. You
will eafily imagine I fpeak not of vices
but follies; thofe little ridiculous follies
of fancy, beyond the borders of cuftom,

tom, to which we are fometimes impel-
led, though fure of making a difgrace-
ful retreat.

I was thinking of Rouffeau this morning as I rambled before breakfaft through
the neighbouring fields. Two or three
little birds were hopping about in the
path. At my approach they fled to a
greater diftance—as I advanced they
fled farther—as I drew ftill nearer they
took fhelter in a hedge. I was concerned.—Why do ye fly me, gentle and apprehenfive creatures? I would not cap-
tivate or injure ye—I would gladly contribute to your felicity. Obferve, thefe
were only my *thoughts,* but mark the
fequel. " Rouffeau," *faid I,* " would
perhaps have *fpoke* to the birds." *Ma-
dam!* cried my attendant. I fmiled at

I 6   my

my own folly, and made fome infignifi-
cant anfwer.

But I need not illuftrate this weaknefs. "Tis fufficient to fay, that I am
very feldom fatisfied with myfelf, and
fhould I, at any future time, perufe
what I am *now* writing, it would moft
probably appear highly cenfurable and
ridiculous.

Pray don't you think, (for I am unwilling to be quite fingular) that my favourite Mr. Shenftone poffeffed a good
deal of this felf-created uneafinefs? I
don't recollect ever hearing you fay
much about him or his writings. Was
he not a good poet? His benevolence
was certainly admirable, and illuminated all his works. I always perufe them
with

with pleafure; with ten times the pleafure than more witty performances would give me. But this, I know, is becaufe of my own deficiencies, not having a fpark of wit, nor a grain of humour in my whole compofition; nor indeed any qualification to entitle me (without great allowance of courtefy) to the honour of being ftyled *your* correfpondent and friend.

To *.*

I AM going to write a long and par-
ticular anfwer to every part of your letter, though at the fame time I have bufinefs of much greater confequence that ought to engage my attention. You

are

are not, however, obliged to me for this civility. I have recourse to it in my own defence, against a set of melancholy ideas, which I hope to dissipate by thus conversing with you; and shall then be more fit for what I could not at present undertake.

But, O frail and insufficient *Humanity!* thou who hast recourse to so many different expedients to support thyself in tolerable serenity, why aspirest thou not more ardently after *celestial* expedients? after the hope that remains steady and immoveable, the tranquillity that fadeth not away!

I think myself obliged, in the first place, by your sitting down to write before my letter came to hand, because

it

it fhews that you thought of me without being reminded.

You have *by this time*, recollected " *who it was*" that his friends complimented, &c. If I were not in a very grave humour, I could fmile at that expreffion.—We are apt now to fancy that fuch a man muft be *happy*. Elegance united with philofophy conveys this idea through the medium of *time*; becaufe we fee not the clouds of perplexity; error, doubt, fear, and forrow that might fecretly over-fhadow his happinefs.

" The cup of felicity pure and unmixed, is by no means a draught for mortal man;" nor can the utmoft perfection of mortality *deferve* it. Sufficient for us, if, with patience and refignation,

W.

we imbibe the intermingled fweets and bitters of our allotted potion, and find *hope* remain at the bottom!

We are fo accuftomed to call things by wrong names, that I am not furprifed at your finding *dulnefs* in a *brilliant* affemblée, and *good* company the *worft* company of all; but you fhould confider by whom and for what end thefe circles are formed. It is very natural for people who are incapable of amufing themfelves to affociate with each other. They feek not *happinefs*, but *amufement*, and *expect* no other fatisfaction than barely employing the time which hangs heavy on their hands. But no more on this fubject—'tis the beaten track of the moralift, and is worn to the very edge.

I come

I come now to your acknowledgment of my letter.—It flatters me—a gleam of fatisfaction enlightens—but why—why did you break off fo abruptly?—Why could you not for *once* intruſt a fincere friend with the *genuine* effuſions of your heart.

How feldom do we difcover to one another our real felves! Cuſtom and education enwrap us in a thouſand difguifes, all more painful to an ingenuous mind, than the European habit to a favage, or fetters to a flave. Nature and fentiment revolt from this tyranny—occafionally they each endeavour to get free—their efforts are vigorous and fudden, agreeing with the impulfe of the paffions.—But referve, who ſtands centinel,

tinel, gives quick alarm, and we continue the flaves of cuftom.

I believe I am writing nonfenfe—my thoughts wander far from the fubject—but 'tis no matter—I fhall write on.

Senfibility, or the characteriftic of a fenfible mind, is a fafhionable and almoft thread-bare topic. Much has been written, much is every day faid about it, and numbers affect to poffefs it, who have no *other* claim than thinking it a recommendation.

This obfervation does not extend to *you*, my fenfible friend, who do, in reality poffefs more than a neceffary fhare. I only mention it, becaufe you are "unwilling to be quite fingular." There

are

are people enough to keep you in countenance, by running into greater abfurdities merely through affectation.

As for Rouffeau, you injure yourfelf
in a comparifon with him. Not that I
accufe him of much affectation, for his
feelings are amazingly ftrong; but he
has fuffered what was once but a re-
fpectable weaknefs, to degenerate into
a fixed habit of difcontent, which is now
the fource of perpetual unhappinefs to
himfelf and others. Your feelings are
as delicate, but lefs irritable than his.
Rouffeau's peculiarity of temper unfits
him for fociety, and confcious of this,
he endeavours to loofen the bands which
hold it together. But his doctrines
make few converts; we difcover inftantly the fpring from which they arife,

and

and are content to let *him* remain *le
folitaire* .. It is fit it fhould be fo. I
cannot help efteeming Rouffeau in fpite
of all his vagaries, and perhaps *for*
fome of them, but I would no more
chufe him for an affociate, than I would
ufe conftantly a fine porcelain veffel, if
its owner ftood as conftantly by, defiring
me not to break it.

I have infenfibly written myfelf into
better fpirits, but muft continue the me-
dicine a little longer.

Pray why did you not *exprefs* your
defire of feeing Rouffeau before he left
us? It might very eafily have been gratified. I fhould have been happy to have
brought you together, and am juft now
diverted by the thoughts of your interview,

view, of which you may take the following for a defcription. Gravely pre-
fenting you to the philofopher, " See,"
I would fay, " Monf. Rouffeau, behold
in this lady -   -   -   -   -   -   -   -

-   -   -   -   -   -   -   -   -   -   -

-   -   -   -   -   -   -   -   -   -   -

-   -   -   -   -   -   -   -   -   -   - ! "   .

Caught by thefe founds, he repeats *O
facred virtue!* and glances a look towards you. Your countenance ftrength-
ens his ideas—the fingularity of his
charaƈter overfpreads it with an attention equally interefting and flattering—
your eyes, enlivened by curiofity and
foftened by complacency, muft *penetrate*
the fufceptible foul of John James. He
cries out! he embraces you with tears
of joy! You become his difciple, and
I, perhaps, lofe my correfpondent.

See,

See, by this inference, that I allow
fomething of a fympathy in your tafte,
though not enough to juftify a comparifon.—What I have now been writing
was to amufe myfelf; but I will tell you
more ferioufly that I knew a chara&er
to which your's bears a much greater refemblance; it is that of the pious and
ingenious Mrs. *Rowe*; nor will you think
it bad counfel, if I advife you to improve the refemblance to perfe&ion.
May your life be as amiable, and your
death as happy!

I have nothing to fay with refpe& to
your *felf-depreçiation*, being unwilling to
charge *you* with the foible of *begging ap-*
plaufe; not that wit and humour are fuch
very eftimable qualities—but I will acquit

quit you—and will believe you are not
fenfible of poffeffing either.

You inquire my opinion of *Shenſtone*,
and his writings.—Good—very good—
you yourſelf have given them a juſt character. I eſteemed—I regretted—I *ſtill*
regret him—and that for more reaſons
than you can poffibly imagine. Alas!
how many worthy people have I out-
lived! I pray God that *you* may never
be added to their number!

Adieu.

To

To *.

THE firſt part of your letter, my ever-honoured, my revered correſpondent, ſhall paſs without notice. I can *ſympathize*, though I do not *inquire*; and whatever were the ideas that diſturbed you, I wiſh not to recall them. Haſtening, therefore, to the paragraph where you beſtow ſuch an unmerited compliment, I acknowledge it moſt gratefully, and am fired with emulation to copy the illuſtrious pattern. How generous, how worthy of yourſelf are thoſe wiſhes in my favour! O may they be anſwered!

I hardly know how to interpret what you ſay about begging applauſe. I hope you *do* acquit me; for indeed I

can acquit *myfelf*, though I readily acknowledge a pleafure and pride in *your*
approbation.

Lætus fum laudari à laudato viro.

Searching for amufement, this morning, among the treafures of your bene-
ficence, I found fome verfes in a poem
of Mr. Whitehead's fo extremely applicable to my thoughts, that I could not
forbear tranfcribing them, and fubjoin-
ing another ftanza, borrowed from two
different authors, to give it the air of a
fonnet.

Yes, I remember, and with pride repeat
  The rapid progrefs which our friendfhip knew!
Even at the firft with willing minds we met,
  And ere the root was fixt the branches grew.
Iu vain had Fortune placed her weak barrier,
  Clear was thy breaft from pride, and mine from
      fervile fear.

            K   I faw

I saw thee generous, and with joy can say,
  My education rose above my birth;
Thanks to those parent shades, on whose cold clay
  Fall fast my tears, and lightly lie the earth!
To them I owe what'er I dare pretend,
Thou saw'st with partial eyes, and bade me call
      thee friend.

And now, while chear'd by thy superior praise,
  I bless the silent path the fates decree,
And from the list of my inglorious days
  Gladly erase the moments crown'd by thee—
O let this boast to future times descend,
Thou wert indeed my guide, my counsellor, my
      friend!

———————

The transcription of these verses
brought on a poetical appetite, which
I gratified immediately by perusing
some *certain pieces* that I hardly durst
venture to speak of, lest I should incur
an imputation that my soul disdains.
                              You

You never fhall accufe me *juftly* of flattery; yet I *muft* fay, in the language
of Plato to Fenelon, " When one reads
your compofitions, one thinks that one
hears Apollo's lyre, ftrung by the hands
of the Graces, and tuned by the
Mufes,"

or rather by Apollo himfelf.

To * *.

A LL praife is foreign, but of true defert,
Plays round the head, but reaches not the heart.
Ah! why recall the toys of thoughtlefs youth ;
When flowery fiction held the place of truth?
When fancy rul'd ; when trill'd each trivial ftrain,
But idly fweet, and elegantly vain.

O!

O! in that ftrain, if all of wit had flow'd,
All mufic warbled, and all beauty glow'd;
Had livelieft nature, happieft art combin'd,
That lent each grace, and this each grace refin'd;
Alas! how little were my proudeft boaft!
The fweeteft trifler of my tribe at moft.

To fway the judgment while he charms the ear;
To curb mad paffion in its wild career;
To blend with fkill, as loftieft themes require;
All reafon's rigour and all fancy's fire;
Be this the poet's praife.—With this uncrown'd,
Wit dies a jeft, and poetry a found.

——— ———

In Mafon's Monody on the death of
Pope you may read this poetical anfwer
to your poëtical epiftle. Adieu.

To

To *.

YOUR poetical reproof, for I can hardly call it a letter, has rather difconcerted me, and made me doubt whether I may purfue my intention, which was to tranfcribe any little occafional piece of poetry that fhould feem applicable to my purpofed fubject. I ever loved to clothe my own thoughts in other people's language; but this is an unneceffary remark; for I am fure you muft often fmile at my frequent quotations, and compare them to *Sancho's* proverbs. They are at leaft as *ready*, and perhaps equally well chofen.

The intended fubject of to-day was a copy of verfes addreffed to my Lord

K 3   Chefter-

Chesterfield, which I found in the Ma-
gazine, and suppose to be lately written.
There is a vein of delicacy runs through
it that softens the hyperbole—in short,
I must transcribe it, and pray do not
throw it into the fire without reading,
but rather (leaving out the allusion to
Lord C.'s misfortune) consider it as ad-
dressed to yourself by

> Your most obliged and obedient.

To the Earl of CHESTERFIELD.

Reclin'd beneath thy shade, *Blackheath!*
　From politics and strife apart,
His temples crown'd with laurel wreath,
　And virtue smiling at his heart;
Will *Chesterfield* the muse allow
　To break upon his still retreat?
To view, if health still smooths his brow,
　And prints his grove with willing feet;

> Though

Though gratitude be rarely found
   In courts or spacious drawing-room,
Still shall she tread poetic ground,
   And favours past shall ne'er intomb.
'Twas this awoke the present theme,
   (And bade it reach thy distant ear)
Where if no ray of genius beam,
   Sincerity at least is there.
May pale disease fly far aloof
   O'er vernal domes its flag display,
And health beneath thy peaceful roof,
   Add lustre to thine evening ray !
If this my fervent wish be crown'd,
   I'll deck with flow'rs the godhead's shrine ;—
Nor thou, with wisdom's chaplet bound,
   At any absent gift repine.
What tho' thou dost not grace a throne
   Where subjects bend the supple knee,
No other king the muses own,
   And science lifts her eye to thee.
Tho' deafness, by a doom severe,
   Steals from thy ear the murm'ring rill,
Or Philomel's delightful air,
   You deem not *this* a partial ill.

K. 4.   Ah !

Ah! if anew thine ear was ſtrung,
  Awake to ev'ry voice around,
Thy praiſes by the many ſung
  Would ſtun thee with the choral ſound!—

To * *.

I AM not very well this morning; I was taken with a ſhivering yeſterday, and had a feveriſh, bad night, but am in hopes it will wear off again. Doctor * at leaſt *bids* me hope ſo, and tells me there is no doubt of it.

I thank you for your verſes; for tho' I had ſeen them long ago, I was pleaſed with the re-peruſal. I was pleaſed too
                                    with

with the fairnefs and elegance of the tranfcript. I admire your *Italiano*.

————'Tis a fair hand:
And whiter than the paper it wrote on
Is the fair hand that writ.————

Thefe verfes reminded me of your *extempore*. It is really very unkind to deny me fo often another fight of it. You don't know how foothing thefe things are at a certain time of life; neither is there any fear that *poetry*, if tolerable, will ever meet an unwelcome reception. The humours of mankind are fo different at different times, that one muft not judge them by a fingle event: befides, the poetical reproof, as you call it, was only fent as a quotation that appofitely anfwered *your* quotation; nor does it intimate the prohibition of

K 5 rhyme,

rhyme, it only reftrains the praife of it. I would have all praife confined to me-ritorious actions. *Virtue* would tire be-fore fhe got to her journey's end, if *Vanity* did not give her a lift now and then; but the more trivial accomplifh-ments fhould be fparingly commended.

For this reafon, and becaufe I hate to fay the fame things inceffantly, I of-ten forbear paying the *due* tribute of civility to my fair correfpondent. My letters would be a mere ftring of pane-gyric, were I to exprefs the juftice my heart does to your good qualities, or even to the common productions of your ingenious *pen*.

And really I was guilty of *ingratitude* as well as neglect, when I forebore ac-knowledging

knowledging your very polite applica-
tion of Mr. Whitehead's verfes, in the
management of which, and the connexion of the other lines, there is more
ingenuity and merit than in many original poems. I fhould be afhamed to
tell you *how much* I was pleafed with
that generous compliment. Abundance
of the fine things which poor mortals
beftow upon one another by way of
praife, are received with coldnefs and
inattention; but what bofom is proof
againft the delicate infinuations of
kindnefs and *efteem?* In fhort, no compliment can be acceptable to a perfon of
merit, though it fhould raife a blufh on
the cheek, unlefs it produce at the fame
time *a glow in the heart.*

K 6   To

To amufe myfelf *and you*, I think I will tranfcribe a few lines, very much in the ftyle of thofe to Lord Chefter-field: they were written before you were born, and appeared firft in the Maga-zines of thofe days.   As you *did not* know the author, I may fay the thought is not inelegantly turned.   *Ecoutez*,

To A LADY.

Written on the Banks of a River near her Father's Villa.

While thefe clofe walls her beauties hide,
    For whofe dear fake forlorn I rove ;
On the clear ftream's oppofing fide
    The Mufe fhall wail my haplefs love.
My love !—which nothing can otuvie,
    Which never fhall a period know;
Ye breezes tell her as ye fly,
    Ye waters bear it as ye flow.—

And

And tho' (by adverfe friends confin'd)
　My yielding fair I vainly crave ;
O bring her murmurs, gentle wind,
　Her image, ev'ry paffing wave !
Ah no !—Ye winds her fighs conceal,
　Nor you, ye waves, refleƈt her face,
Left Æolus my paffion feel,　.
　And Neptune fue for her embrace.
Small need ye fhould her accents bear,
　Or to my view her form impart,
Whofe voice dwells ever on my ear,
　Whofe image ever in my heart.

———

Adieu for the prefent ; I am obliged
to break off, but will add a few lines
anon.

———

You will be forry to hear that I left
off through indifpofition. My diforder

is

is increafed. It is with difficulty that I write—but this will be in time three hours hence; fo I can fend you a later account.

————————

I was not able to refume in time for the Diligence; fo Difpatch fhall carry you this, and fatisfy all your enquiries.

I. *really* am extremely ill; and fancy myfelf worfe for not having ..... yet why repine ..... Many there are with *equal* propenfities to domeftic tendernefs who are denied the fweets of it. Per-haps the exalted fhare I once partook .... but away with thefe ufelefs com-plainings .... yet 'tis natural at the inftant of fuffering to wifh relief.

My

My prefent wifh is for the fociety of a kindred mind. Why fhould I not fay for *your* fociety, my amiable friend? for *your* foothing converfation. You are capable of generous fympathy ... You would fuffer my drooping head to re-pofe on your gentle bofom .... You would fhed the tear of compaffion on my pale cheek .... and above all, you would defire, in the words of your ad-mirable motto, which I have been con-templating this half hour, I fay, you would defire with *fincerity* that I fhould

" *Live a little longer.*"

Adieu. Pardon this weaknefs ... I will conquer it .... Adieu.

To

To *.

WHAT can I fay to your letter?
—O my friend! And are you
really fo much indifpofed!—I am diftracted with grief and apprehenfion—
perhaps you are worfe by this time—
yet God forbid! Write inftantly, I conjure you—on my knees I conjure you
to write inftantly: and if you wifh for
my company—but, alas! what fervice
can I render?—yet fay the word—fhall
I come?—If you defire it I will come
—regardlefs of fame, regardlefs of cenfure—happy, too happy, if my care,
my affiduity, my unwearied and affectionate attention, can procure you one
moment's fatisfaction.—What *can* I fay?
—*You* fhall determine for me.—I cannot

not write.—God Almighty reſtore you to health; or I know not what will become of your Friend.

———————————————

To * *.

I RECEIVED your's more than thirty hours ago, and have waited till now for an interval of eaſe to anſwer it, being deſirous of expreſſing myſelf as fully as poſſible.

Do not be ſurpriſed .... or ſhocked ... if I tell you ... that the doctors have juſt left me ... with compliments on what they were pleaſed to call the *magnanimity* of their patient.

And

And does it then require greatnefs of mind, to hear with tranquillity a fentence that one ought hourly to expect—or rather their prognoftic of that fentence? Perhaps fo—but it may be that *my* compofure arifes from a doubt of their prefaging fkill: I feel at leaft a firmnefs of *hope* that feems to contradict their opinion ..... Yes .... I will tell you, (though 'tis too ftriking a proof of human frailty) that I ftill *hope* to recover.

Be that as it may, I was determined to feize the opportunity of writing, and reftoring your letters. I inclofe even the laft, for the contents are engraven on my heart. Nor let this precaution alarm you—it is no argument of danger —I may recover—I may write again— again I may thank you for the pleafures

your

your friendſhip has afforded.—But if not—who ſhall diſpute the decrees of Providence !

In this caſe, remember that (in the Biſhop of Lucon's words to Madame de Rouvraie) " I make it my laſt requeſt, that you will not grieve overmuch for the loſs of the ſincereſt friend that ever had being; and yet not worthy of a friend like you." Preſerve for my memory an affectionate, a *friendly* regard; but if ever you cheriſhed in my favour *the very ſlighteſt degree* of a more tender ſentiment, transfer it with *addition* to ſome deſerving perſon, and confirm your gift at the altar. It is my ſerious and deliberate advice that you will not paſs the prime of your life in an unconnected ſtate. You are formed

to

to fhine in the domeftic circle, to receive and impart the very effence of
conjugal happinefs.   Commit to fome
worthy man the charge of your felicity.
May he endeavour as fincerely to promote it as I myfelf would have done,
had the envied and too ardently wifhed-
for office been attainable.   However ill-
timed this declaration may be thought,
it is no more than what every I
cannot proceed . . . I am extremely ill
. . . Adieu.

———

A fhort interval feems afforded . . . .
I embrace it to finifh this letter and remove your friendly anxiety—or at leaft
that uneafy *fufpenfe* with which I am
vain enough to think your mind is agitat-
ed.

ed.—At fuch a feafon as this, can I add felfifhnefs to vanity?—can I tell you that I derive comfort from your bene-volent forrow? Yes, I *muft* tell you that the idea (fuggefted by your laft) of your unfeigned regard, is a cordial to my very foul!

Again I muft paufe through inability .... the pen drops from my hand ...

I would by no means have you think of coming hither—nor did I expect you to make the generous offer. I com-plained of being debarred your com-pany, but did not folicit you to grant it. Your fame is, and was ever, as dear to me as your friendfhip; and when I

confider

confider the true nature and extreme delicate texture of female honour, I regret not the facrifices I have made to it, nor even that I let your opinion prevail againft the *bequeft.*

Adieu.   I cannot perfuade myfelf that this is the laft time of addrefling you; but left it fhould ... I fend you my beft wifhes ...... God Almighty protect, fuftain, preferve, and blefs you ... here and for ever!

Adieu, my tender, my fincere friend. —Deareft and moft amiable of women —Adieu.

To

To the fame.

I LIVE.——I am recovering—and the fecond effort of my pen is to acquaint you with it. The firft was dedicated to that POWER which beftowed the ability; and the *enclofed* contains my fentiments on the occafion. You muft however return it uncopied.—No eye but your's and the ALL-SEEING fhall ever behold it. Be pleafed alfo to ufe caution in giving your opinion of this hafty production. Faults it doubtlefs may have; but not fuch as will warrant criticifm. You now perhaps think I refemble the archbifhop in *Gil Blas*; and that my indifpofition having weakened the mental powers, I am no more capable

pable of judging than of writing—but I only intended to obferve, that an effufion of gratitude or tranfport fhould not be tried by the rules of colder compofitions. On the other hand, you muft by no means *commend* it; for whatever degree of merit it poffeffes, is in reality detracted from *my* character. Every ardent expreffion conveys a fecret reproof; and the general tenor of it is a reproach to a man who has at times affected to be weary of the gift which it celebrates, and ought rather to have been prepared to *refign* it with equal cheerfulnefs.

Yet who, to dumb forgetfulnefs a prey,
　This pleafing anxious being e'er refign'd,
Left the warm precincts of the cheerful clay,
　Nor caft one longing ling'ring look behind.

I am

I am now impatient to receive the congratulations that your gentle and friendly heart will dictate upon this occasion. Difpatch, who travels all night, will call again for your anfwer. From him too you may learn more particularly the circumftances of my amendment. I am ftill very faint and languid, but while returning health fmiles within my view, I can eafily fupport fo trivial an inconvenience.

Adieu. I rejoice to fubfcribe myfelf yet once again your friend—your fincere and very affectionate friend.

Is not this a very good opportunity to folicit a copy of the *extempore* verfes that I have fo often requefted in vain?

L.   Surely

Surely you will not know how to refuse me juft now. I fhall expect to fee them inclofed with the Ode.

To *.

YOU are impatient to receive the congratulations that my heart ftill dictate on this occafion, and moft probably expect more from me than you will receive, for the language of *my heart* is not expreffibly, nor could any degree of eloquence convey an idea of its joy. I blefs and adore the goodnefs of that *Being* whofe favour has reftored you to health ; and befeech him to keep you for ever in his holy protection—but why

fhould

fhould I attempt to tell *you* how fincerely I rejoice;—how fervently I wifh
you long life and happinefs? The warm-
eft profeffions are no more than empty
founds, and might be ufed by the moft
indifferent perfon.

> If wifhing well had but a body in it
> That might be felt, then, we the poorer born,
> Whofe bafer ftars do fhut us up in wifhes
> Might with effects of them follow our friends.

But as it is, I will only defire you to de-
lineate in your fancy the fincereft and
moft ardent effufion of tendernefs and
friendfhip, and believe that it fprings
from my heart.

I return you the Ode with a thoufand
acknowledgments, and *uncopied* too, but

in

in " the volume of my brain." I dare not give my opinion—you would ac-cufe me of flattery—neither could any panegyric—but I will not fay a word about it.

Enclofed with this inimitable piece, O Heavens, what an unworthy com-panion!—You will find the *extempore*, which at length (though reluctantly) I fubmit to your perufal, becaufe " *I knew not how to refufe.*"

Upon fecond thoughts, I will not en-clofe, but tranfcribe it, *in this place*, for I protefted (if you remember) that it fhould never go out of my hand---but I will copy it *verbatim & literatim*.

When

When pleafure thrills through ev'ry vein,
    And trembling nerves confefs its fway,
How hard to pen the meafur'd ftrain!
    But *you* command and I obey.
And *** fhould be my theme—
    But he, alas, is now too near,
Nor in his prefence can I frame
    A verfe to pleafe his critic ear.
My heart with gratitude oppreft,
    Would fain its honeft tribute pay,
But whilft I *fee* my honour'd gueft,
    The pow'rs of language fhrink away.
When Phœbus darts his noon-tide beam,
    We ne'er to fing his praife afpire,
O'erpower'd by glory's fervid ftream,
    We pant; and drop the filent lyre.
But when he finks behind the hill,
    And paints with radiance *diftant* fkies,
Our frefhen'd fouls exert their fkill,
    And hymns in cheerful chorus rife.

L 3   O par-

O pardon then my languid mufe,
  As thefe unpolifh'd lines you view,
And own they merit fome excufe   .
  For being wrote to pleafure you.

————

I fhould tell you, my noble friend,
that I have been much indifpofed myfelf within this week paft—a kind of fe-
verifh complaint—with lofs of reft and
appetite—but am now greatly amended,
and going for the firft time to take an
airing. The chaife is at the door.—
Perhaps I may fetch Mr. ** to dine
with me—but I need not apologize, for
my letter is fufficiently long when the
fubfcription is added—which, if I knew
how to compofe it, fhould be as refpect-
ful—as affectionate—as joyful—but ah !
—*c'eft impoffible*—Adieu.   Adieu.

To

To * *.

YOUR gratulation, my amiable friend, fell not fhort of the demand my fancy had made on it—it exceeding that demand, and has laid me under frefh obligations.

I admire your difclaiming the help of eloquence at the inftant that you practife the moft refined fpecies of it. What think you of the *break* in your concluding fentence? or even the fimple repetion of the word *adieu?* 'Tis thefe kind of ftrokes that, through an underftanding ear, produce the moft powerful effects. Let me tell you, in the language of Shakefpeare, " You do fpeak mafterly." Your expreffions are fo touching—fo tender—

L 4 They

They give a very echo to the feat
Where love is thron'd.————

I perufe them every hour in the day,
and always with increafing pleafure.

O you that have a heart of fuch fine frame
To pay this debt of love but to a *friend*,
How would you love—if *Cupid*'s potent fhaft—

Would to Heaven the trial could be
made!

————

5 o'Clock,
I left off abruptly this morning, and
ought to apologize for the levity of my
concluding line; but you will excufe it
—you cannot be difpleafed with a cheerfulnefs that fprings from the return of
health, and which, I hope, you will
foon increafe by an account of your
own

own perfect recovery. Shall I add——
No, I will not——I will for ever ba-
nifh from my heart the fuggeftions of
a vanity fo intolerable—and I beg you
never to defire an explanation of this.
fentence.

Let me inform you, my good friend,
(for you are poffibly ignorant) what is
the chief merit of my letters. 'Tis their
incoherency. A ftrange recommendation, but one that proclaims them the
effufion of the *moment*, which ought to
be the characteriftic of all familiar writing.   :

And pray now, let me inquire (for I
have often intended it) what becomes of
my letters ... Do you preferve or
deftroy them? Methinks I have a cu-

riofity

riofity to know what I have been saying to you this year and a half, but more particularly within thefe fix months. God knows I very feldom take the pains of reading what I write to you, left any ftriking tautology fhould induce me to *correct* or *tranfcribe*.——Apropos to tranfcription—let me thank you a thoufand times for the *extempore*. The moment I caft my eyes on it, I fmiled at difcovering in two particular lines (which had efcaped my memory) the *abfolute* reafon of your unwillingnefs to part with it. Come now—what wager? —but this is not generous—pardon me —I accept it very gratefully upon your own term, and will copy it myfelf.

I have no thoughts of coming to town at prefent.—My movements, in general, are

are very uncertain. It will, perhaps, be a long time ere we meet, but when we do, I shall most probably say with *Iáchimo*, " I'd make a journey twice as far, &c."—Adieu. I know not how to conclude.—Write, write *soon*, I beseech you!

To *.

EXCEPTING two or three on particular subjects, as the counsel's instruction, &c. I have no letters of your's, my Lord, but what are of this year's date. I destroyed the rest; but have preserved all these in a series, beginning with one that I wrote on New-Year's-Day. I have numbered them

L 6 according

according to the dates, and having erafed every fyllable that could gratify impertinent curiofity, I keep them very fecurely in my cabinet, and intended not to review them till after Chriftmas; —however they fhall at any time obey your fummons.

But there are certain reflections fuggefted by the contents of your laft favour, that almoft induce me to wifh I had never engaged fo heartily in this correfpondence. Freedom, unreferve, were the propofed conditions—and I *have* wrote freely—fo freely—that—in. fhort—I don't much like to recollect *how* freely.—Not that I repent of having exprefled—any thing that *is* exprefled.—The refinement of delicacy, I know, is incompatible with familiar writing
ing

ing—Indeed our fex has very little bufinefs with familiar writing. It generally
creates embarraffments of one kind or
other—but I thought my fituation and
circumftance exempted—I don't know
what I would fay—my very ftyle is per-
plexed. The meaning of it all is an apprehenfion of having fuffered in your
opinion, through a fuppofed want of delicacy or proper referve.

Neverthelefs I had rather (if you
pleafe) decline entering into any difqui-
fition of the fubject. It is a caufe that
will not bear examination; and I beg
that my acquittal of this charge (if I
am acquitted) may pafs in filence, which
I fhall regard as a fufficient juftification,
and begin immediately upon a new
fcore.

After

After the many obligations you have conferred, I cannot doubt of this being added to the number, and am, &c.

<hr>

To * *.

I WILL fpare you " the *examination* of this caufe," and would have readily granted the whole of your requeft, had you not talk'd of " beginning a new fcore if acquitted in *filence*."

Let us have no new fcores, I befeech you.—My age is a very improper one for beginning new leffons, and a very fufficient reafon for continuing the old.

"An

" An apprehenfion of having fuffered in your opinion through a fuppofed want of delicacy or proper referve." Ah! my good friend, of what
texture is this newly affumed veil, that,
without difguifing, attracts a clofer obfervation. You knew *my* opinion better; but you were afraid of fuffering
in *your own* for certain expreffions—
(the truth muft come out; I gave you
a hint of it about the extempore) for
certain expreffions of *kindnefs* that had
dropt unawares from your pen.————
" Don't much like to recollect"————
Indeed.—You are afhamed then of having expreffed kindnefs for a benevolent
old man, who regards you with paternal
affection.

Are

Are you aware of the inference that ——but I ſpare you—becauſe you have not ſuffered nor ever can " ſuffer in my opinion through ſuppoſed want of delicacy," or even " the refinement of delicacy."

In a letter wrote during my illneſs, I remember diſcloſing my ſentiments with a freedom that I thought became the occaſion. Has this openneſs created a diſtance between us? It ought not. To the beſt of my remembrance, I told you, with great ſimplicity, that I preferred you, in all reſpeſts, to all women; and had deſtiny permitted, would have gladly *evinced* that declaration; but is this a reaſon for your drawing back as it were, and witholding the marks of an eſteem of which I am *not*

p ermitted

permitted to avail myfelf? Why do you force me to be unpolite? Why do you oblige me to declare that I am proof againft all your attra&tions; that I never can become your lover; and that, *there-fore*, your delicacy can never be impeached, or your referve acquitted?

What can I fay more to fatisfy you? From the firft moment of our acquaintance, I marked you down as a fubje&t of examination (my ufual method when tempted to form a friendfhip) and you have not yet failed in the trial. I have ftudied your difpofition; I have fathomed your capacity; I have tried your temper ... I have weighed, in the balance of impartiality, your virtues and your foibles. How do the former preponderate! Let me entreat you not to throw

a fcruple

a fcruple into the oppofite fcale. In a word, I have feen you at all hours, in all dreffes, in all companies, and have obferved a uniform, an *invariable* delicacy prefide over your whole conduct.

Do thefe acknowledgments anfwer your demand? or will you ftill difqualify, and ftill folicit applaufe? Pardon this laft expreffion—'tis too fevere. I had forgot the influence that diffident modefty has over confcious merit; and yet I cannot conclude without telling you, in very plain language, my fixed determination.

The abfurd and ridiculous cuftoms of the world we inhabit, makes it neceffary (in fome degree) for us to live apart, Deprived of your converfation, I am

folaced

folaced by your familiar correfpondence. If you over-fhadow *this* with
unneceffary referve, I will exchange it
for the other, and become, in fpite of
oppofition, your inceffant vifitor. Chufe,
therefore, one of thefe alternatives, and
abide by your choice. Believe me, I
had much rather be your gueft than your
correfpondent, and when I recollect my
laft vifit to ***, I can never forbear *wifhing* to repeat it.

That vifit——You know not, my dear
Mrs. **, how many circumftances, how
many agreeable reflections——The
moon-light in the garden—Do you remember it?—Twas in croffing the little
lawn near the houfe that we ftopt fhort
to admire the beauty of the fcene, and
liften, more attentively to the concealed
mufic

mufic that vibrated along the hedges.
Your hand was within my arm .... It
had felt the preffure of my lips ....
You withdrew it ..... Have you forgot
that moment? ... *I never* fhall forget it.
Apprehenfive delicacy forbad thofe natural, innocent, filent expreffions of fatisfaction; whilft VIRTUE, in *your* accents, directed our eyes and our thoughts
to the ftarry heavens, and almoft enabled
them to penetrate the azure canopy.
What an apoftrophe! What fublimity!
What tendernefs! O had the excellent
creature to whom ..... but no more,
left 1 injure the fubject. This was indeed one of thofe precious and unfre-
quent moments, when, by a happy con-
currence of circumftances, Humanity
feems raifed above itfelf, and feels fenfations of which the vulgar, the ignorant,

rant, or the licentious mind cannot form
an idea!

I have been reading what I have
written, and am pleafed with my un-
premidated digreffion. I hope it will
not *difpleafe* my fair reader. Come,
come, my dear friend, for fo I will call
you, think better of this matter. Dif-
card affe&ation. Return my *fincere* my
difinterefted affe&ion with *equal* fincerity
and franknefs. The journey of life is,
with me, drawing faft to a conclufion.
Short indeed is the remaining paffage;
but rugged to the feet of a weary tra-
veller, and barren to his decaying fight.
Continue then, to beguile the irkfome-
nefs of the way, footh him with the fong
of

of fympathy, and ftrew the flowers of friendfhip in his path.

———— ——

Wednefday.

This will be a moft unreafonable let-ter, for a frefh fubject has offered, and one that I have *intended* at leaft twenty times to mention, and it has always efcaped me: *Junius*, and his writings. Pray what is your opinion of them, par-ticularly the laft letter? I am fure his reprefentations muft intereft you a little; but you fhould diftinguifh the matter from the manner, and hear both fides of the queftion, before you decide on the merits of this popular writer.

I think now that this is a very *oppor-tune* change of our fubject. Let us then,

if

if you pleafe, drop entirely all difcourfe of ourfelves, our fituation, our fentiments, and commence politicians without lofs of time. Take no notice of *the firft part of this letter*, but acquaint me, as foon as poffible, with all your political notions, and, in Quidnunc's language, " *What you take to be the balance of power.*"

But firft you muft let me know— though that is needlefs too; for I'll be fworn you are a *Patriot*, a true daughter of Britain ; " *always for liberty.*"

> No love but that of Carthage fires my bofom.
> —————————for thee, O what for thee,
> My finking country, would I not endure !

Ay, ay, fhe did *endure*. She deferted the fortunes of a decrepid old hufband

who

who was indifferent to her, and threw herſelf .... not from the top of a precipice .... nor into a cauldron of boiling oil .... but .... O unparalleled ſacrifice .... ſhe threw herſelf ..... into the arms of a handſome young man whom ſhe loved! Poor Sophoniſba! Do you not ſympathize in her ſufferings?

Raillery apart, I beg you will give me your free opinion of this celebrated writer and his compoſitions. I ſhall not influence your judgment by any previous remarks, nor add another line after bidding you very heartily

Farewell.

Thurſday morning.
An unexpected delay obliges me to break my word; but Diſpatch ſhall
bring

bring you this, and inform you what a droll accident has befallen the Diligence. I enclofe your two laſt letters to be numbered and claſſed with the reſt, and then be pleaſed to make them all up in a pacquet for him to bring me hither. I want to review, at my leiſure, this little ſeries of billet-doux, nor will you, I hope ...... but hold—I had like to have infringed our newly eſtabliſhed law, which is, to ſay nothing of ourſelves at preſent, but as much as we pleaſe on any other topic.

I have already *given* you a topic from which. I expeƈt great entertainment. Spread your intellectual pinions, and ſoar at once into the region of politics, ſinging IO *Junius.*

M   To

To *.

I WANTED Difpatch to come for the pacquet in his return from town, as it could make but a few miles differ- ence; but he pleads your commands to the contrary; fo I fhall only detain him while " *I write thefe few lines,*" and ad- juft the other letters.

The *extorted* commendations and cor- rective raillery of this laft favour makes me extremely willing to obferve your " newly-eftablifhed law," and " drop all difcourfe of ourfelves;" though at the fame time I muft affure you, upon my word and honour, that my meaning was not rightly interpreted; nor did I think that the " beginning a new fcore" would be be underftood as a deviation from our ufual plan of writing; but let all that pafs. I have now another tafk allotted me, and fhall engage in it very cheerfully, if you will but hold out the proper lights, and condefcend to be my political preceptor. I fancy I have not feen the laft letter of Junius. Pray mention in your next who it is addreffed to. I fhall for feveral reafons be rather impatient till I have the honour of hearing from you. I am forry for the poor Diligence, though the accident was truly ludicrous; and fhall be glad to refume the more eligible conveyance.

There was no forbearing to laugh at your ridicule of poor Sophonifba's *fecond marriage*; but you take no notice

M 2. of

of the poifon that was her nuptial prefent, nor of her courage in drinking it.
I don't mean (like the young ftudent in
Emilius) on account of its naufeous tafte,
but at all events, and moftly according
to *your* reprefentation of the affair, it
required fome magnanimity.

You know very well that I am jealous of my fex's honour; and there are
feveral *other* paffages in your letter,
which, notwithftanding the prohibition
—but 'tis no matter.—Be affured only,
that I abhor affectation as much as in-
delicacy, and am forry for having fhewn
any *appearance* of it. Your reproofs are
indeed *fevere*, but I will profit by them,
and intreat you, my honoured friend,
never to fpare my foibles. You fhall

not

not find me incorrigible. I do acknowledge that I was to blame (though not
perhaps in the identical inftance or degree that you apprehend) and now having, *as you very juftly obferve,* no *reafon*
for difguifing my fentiments, I *avow*
them, and proclaim myfelf

  Your obliged

   and moft affectionate Friend.

F I N I S.

www.ingramcontent.com/pod-product-compliance
Lightning Source LLC
Chambersburg PA
CBHW022006050726
47499CB00006BB/1941